"What's a nice guy like you doing fooling around with finite equations?"

"What's a nice girl like you doing fooling around with murder?" Dan gave Susan a teasing look. "I'd never guess to look at you that you wrote about blunt instruments and other lethal weapons."

"Arsenic, actually."

"Dare I use the word *trite*?"

"Certainly not! Cyanide is trite. At any rate, the murder in my book took place fifty years ago. So it has to be an old poison."

Dan studied her closely. If this woman was up to something, he'd have to reform her, that's all. He couldn't let her get away from him. "You should be raising orchids, not murdering people in print."

Susan gazed into Dan's eyes. No matter what he said, she didn't believe his story about being a math teacher! But she was falling for Dan...fast! How could she love a man she didn't really know?

Dear Reader:

Happy Holidays! All the best wishes to you for a joyful, loving holiday season with your family and friends.

And while celebrating, I hope that you think of Silhouette Romance. Our authors join me in wishing you a wonderful holiday season, and we have some treats in store for you during November and December—as well as during the exciting new year.

Experience the magic that makes the world so special for two people falling in love. Meet heroines that will make you cheer for their happiness and heroes (be they the boy next door or a handsome, mysterious stranger) that will win your heart. Silhouette Romances reflect the magic of love—sweeping you away with books that will make you laugh and cry, heartwarming, poignant stories that will move you time and time again.

During the next months, we're publishing romances by many of your all-time favorites such as Diana Palmer, Brittany Young, Lucy Gordon and Victoria Glenn. Your response to these authors and others in Silhouette Romances has served as a touchstone for us, and we're pleased to bring you more books with Silhouette's distinctive medley of charm, wit and—above all—*romance*.

I hope you enjoy this book and the many stories to come. Come home to Silhouette Romance—for always!

Sincerely,

Tara Hughes
Senior Editor
Silhouette Books

JOAN SMITH

After the Storm

Published by Silhouette Books New York
America's Publisher of Contemporary Romance

SILHOUETTE BOOKS
300 E. 42nd St., New York, N.Y. 10017

ISBN: 0-373-08617-2

First Silhouette Books printing December 1988

JOAN SMITH

has written many Regency romances, but likes working with the greater freedom of contemporaries. She also enjoys mysteries and Gothics, collects Japanese porcelain and is a passionate gardener. A native of Canada, she is the mother of three.

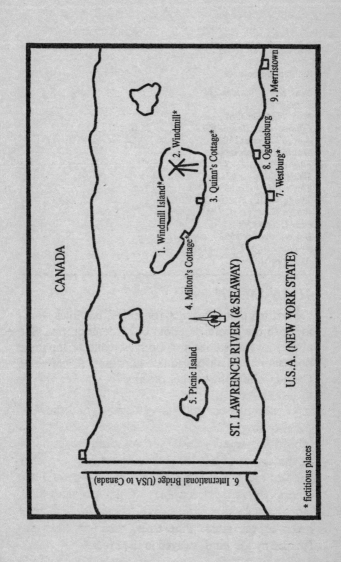

CANADA

ST. LAWRENCE RIVER (& SEAWAY)

U.S.A. (NEW YORK STATE)

1. Windmill Island*
2. Windmill*
3. Quinn's Cottage*
4. Milton's Cottage*
5. Picnic Island
6. International Bridge (USA to Canada)
7. Westburg*
8. Ogdensburg
9. Merristown

* fictitious places

Chapter One

So this is the Thousand Islands!" Susan exclaimed. "I think I'm going to like it here."

Riding in the open boat was like being in a hurricane. The marauding wind seemed to catch her words and throw them back at her. It whipped her black hair around her face as the launch sped along the St. Lawrence River. On all sides sparkled the vast expanse of island-dotted green water.

The islands' amorphous forms suggested those of prehistoric amphibians. One elongated curl of land looked like a giant lizard's tail. Another, hunched low in the water, resembled a bloated frog. The islands were of all shapes and sizes but primarily were two colors: layered outcroppings of sun-bleached limestone added variety and rugged beauty to the gentler green of the grass. Pine trees, their branches deformed by the wind, swayed in the breeze.

Susan's driver, Jed McClean, was a local handyman. Middle-aged, taciturn, he seemed inured to the beauty of the scenery.

"Which one's Windmill Island?" Susan asked.

Jed pointed a weathered finger straight ahead, to their destination. In the distance a tall, narrow windmill that was perched on a rocky promontory formed an exclamation mark against the sky. Susan felt a stab of disappointment. She'd been picturing an old wooden structure that she could actually enter and climb stairs to the top, but its steel grill looked more like the girders of a skyscraper under construction.

As the boat drew closer, Susan could distinguish every detail of the windmill. Its arms were motionless. She knew that several years earlier the owners of the island had had a diesel generator installed. A big black crow perched on one of the arms mocked the windmill's obsolete technology.

The island was long and rose to a limestone peak at the near end. Jed veered the boat to the left and continued past the peak and then past a white frame building with a red roof. A little later he cut the motor and turned the launch sharply toward shore. "This is your aunt's cottage," he said.

He docked at a wooden jetty and helped Susan out. "I'll take the gear up to the cottage, Miss Knight," he said. "Miss Milton wants me to meet her at six on the mainland. You won't be afraid here alone for a few hours till your aunt comes?"

"Of course not," Susan replied, and hopped nimbly onto the dock. "I'll take my own cases. You have enough to carry."

"The wife's been in to tidy up. There's supper waiting for you and Miss Milton. Nell will be over again in the morning to look after you, same as usual."

"Thanks. That will help."

Jed took an armload of luggage to the cottage, and Susan remained behind, getting her bearings. About twenty feet inland sat a stone house that was two stories high, perfectly symmetrical, with windows on either side of the doorway. It looked out of place, plopped down in the wilderness. The only evidence for its being a cottage, rather than a formal house, were the screened-in porch and the hand-painted sign above the doorway: Sans Souci. It was French for "without a care," "carefree."

And that was exactly the kind of vacation she was anticipating. This summer was her reward for a year of working for her aunt. Having just returned from a hectic visit to England, Susan was looking forward to this time away from the heat and the hurly-burly of summer in New York. Of course, she'd have her work to save her from monotony.

Susan felt she'd gone to heaven when her mother's sister offered her the job. Anna had always been her favorite relative—Anna Milton, the celebrated mystery writer. Susan found it hard to believe Anna was really her mom's sister. Their lives were worlds apart. The Knights lived in comfortable anonymity in Philadelphia, where Susan's father ran his own electrical shop. They were perfectly happy there, though Susan's mother looked a little wistful when she got letters postmarked Paris or Rome, but mostly she was so proud of her sister that she forgot to be jealous.

During Anna's visits to Philadelphia, she had always fostered a special closeness with her niece. Unmarried with no children of her own, Anna seemed to have mentally "adopted" Susan Knight. When Susan had graduated from high school, Anna had offered to send her to college, adding gratitude to Susan's admiration. When Susan finally graduated from college, her aunt had offered her the dream job as her secretary. Life had been a merry-go-round ever since.

Susan wanted to be a writer and in her free time had finally finished her first manuscript. Anna had promised to read *Old Lover's Ghost* carefully and suggest improvements.

Jed came back for the last of the boxes, and Susan followed him partway up the path to the house. The stillness all around charmed her. The only sounds were the light hissing of the waves on the shore and the gentle sighing of the pines.

While she was still reveling in the peace, Jed came out. "If there's nothing else, Miss Knight, I'll get back to shore."

"I guess that takes care of everything, then. Thanks, Mr. McClean." He left, and Susan entered the cottage, which seemed dark after the brilliant sunlight.

Now that she was away from the water and the trees, she suddenly found the silence overpowering. She stood in the dim hallway, looking from the living room to the study. Motes of dust floated serenely in shafts of sunbeams.

Susan took a quick tour of the downstairs and found the decor to be typical of a cottage. The living room was paneled in pine, with chintz sofas and rustic wood tables. Next she went to the office, which was whitewashed and had two book-lined walls for her to explore later at her leisure. Louvered shutters were pulled back to admit the sunlight. The big cubbyhole desk must be Anna's. Assigning the table in the corner to herself, Susan put the portable typewriter there, then went on to explore the good-size dining room. The kitchen, across the hall, had all the modern amenities, even a dishwasher.

The next item of interest was her bedroom. She ran upstairs. The largest room, done in chic black and gray and burgundy, had Anna written all over it. Susan assumed she could have her pick of the others and chose one that faced the river. The bedroom was modest but had a stunning view of the water and the mainland, a greenish-gray haze in the distance. Anna had told her this area was part of the St. Lawrence Seaway, the inland water route from the Atlantic to the heartland of America. Susan found it strange to think of this seemingly isolated spot being an international meeting place for ships.

Susan glanced at her watch. Four-thirty. Her aunt should be here by six. Anna had been autographing books in the nearby town of Potsdam and had dropped her niece and the luggage off at the Mc-Clean's on the way. Susan knew Anna would come in, smiling after another successful autographing session, and say, "Is there anything to drink? My throat's parched from saying thank-you. People are *so* kind."

With a little smile of anticipation, Susan ran downstairs and began to arrange the office. She checked that the cellular phone had been installed. Anna had cadged this extravagance from her publisher, since the island didn't have phone service. By the time Susan

had set up the office, it was five o-clock. She decided
to see what Nell McClean had left for dinner. A cas-
serole of chicken cacciatore, already cooked, was in
the fridge, ready to be heated.

To pass the time remaining, she went upstairs and
unpacked her suitcase. At five forty-five, the silence
and waiting were beginning to pall, so she decided to
go outdoors and explore a bit. Just as she headed for
the door, the phone rang.

"Susan, it's Anna. You'll never guess whom I ran
into at Potsdam. Nathan Hanover, the celebrated
science-fiction writer. He was signing there today, too.
Such a charmer. He's invited me out to dinner."

"Tonight?" Susan asked with a wrench of regret.

"Yes, I'm still at Potsdam, calling from a little bar
there. I'll be along to the island around nine. Don't
wait dinner for me. Is everything all right?"

"It's fine. Rather quiet—"

"How I look forward to that! Oh, while I think of
it, Susan, you'd better give Jed McClean a call and tell
him I'll be late. I'll get the boat from the marina and
drive myself over. No reason to take him away from
his family at night. I'll see you around nine. Take
care."

"Bye, Anna."

Susan hung up the phone and breathed a long sigh.
She found Jed's phone number in the directory and
called him. By now it was six o'clock—she had three
more hours alone on the island to enjoy the peace and
quiet. There was plenty of time for her to do that exploring before sundown.

Outside, clouds had begun to darken the sky. Susan did her exploring along the shore. Behind the

house were narrow footpaths into the bush, but she decided to follow them tomorrow. She walked east, toward the white cottage with the red roof, hoping to find a friendly face. There was no boat, nor any sign of life. Was she actually alone on this island? *All* alone? A sudden tremor shook her. It was a strange feeling, being completely cut off from the world.

What if something happened? What if she had an attack of appendicitis? There was always the cellular phone. Susan turned back toward Sans Souci, walking more quickly. She ran the last few yards to the house and locked the door behind her. Her heart was pounding. What was she afraid of? she asked herself. What could possibly happen on an isolated island? There was nobody there to attack her. The silence seemed to mock her.

Susan spoke out loud, just to hear a human voice. "Don't be an idiot," she said sternly. "You've just got a case of jitters. Turn on the oven. Eat your chicken."

By eight she'd eaten her supper, stacked the dishes in the dishwasher and discovered that the TV showed only one program: a snowstorm. The obvious thing to do was to read for an hour. Now that the darkness was closing in, she felt as if she were on display in the lit room, so she decided to close the shutters. She peered out into the shadows. The darkness beyond was dense. That strange impression of a man's shoulders moving was only a bush, she told herself. What else could it be? She pulled the shutters closed and returned to the bookshelves.

At random she picked up a mystery, *Shades of Black*, and by sheer perverse coincidence, it began with a chapter about a girl alone in a house at night, being stalked by a murderer. Susan set the book aside nonchalantly, refusing to admit even to herself that her vague sense of danger had heightened to outright fear. She strained her ears to distinguish the unfamiliar sounds of island life. The wind was rising. She'd seen the bushes outside the window move earlier, and now the tall pines were beginning to groan as their branches were pushed to and fro.

Sitting here, thinking, was bad for her nerves. She decided to prepare the drink tray for Anna's arrival. In the kitchen she made a ritual of arranging glasses, scotch and soda for Anna, Tom Collins with a splash of gin for herself. She'd take care of the ice later, but she got the ice bucket. When the chore couldn't be prolonged anymore, she took the tray to the office.

Now what could she do? Maybe the TV had stopped snowing. She was fiddling with the knobs when the lights went out and she was plunged into darkness. This wasn't the darkness of a city apartment at night, with streetlights beaming through windows. It was an utter, impenetrable blackness, like being buried alive. A gasp of terror escaped her lips. She got up carefully, as though a sudden rush of movement might precipitate some nameless disaster. She stood rigid, every sense alert. There was no sound but the echo of her heartbeat pounding in her ears.

Anna had told her that the generator was unreliable. Were there any candles? Yes! On the dining room table! With a jolt of relief, Susan headed for the dining room. Please let there be matches beside the candlesticks, she prayed. She felt her way along the pitch-black corridor to the dining room. As her eyes adjusted to the darkness, the pale luminescence from the windows was enough for her to locate the candles in crystal holders. There had to matches somewhere.

Susan groped her way to the built-in china cabinet and pulled the top drawer open. A box of safety matches was the first thing she touched. She seized them joyfully and lit the candles. The room leaped into sudden view, showing her a kerosene lamp on a side table. She took off the lamp's chimney and lit the wick.

A steadier, brighter light dispelled the gloom and the terror. When Susan glanced at the mirror over the table, she was surprised to see she was smiling. One would never know from looking at the woman in the mirror that she'd been acting like a child for the past fifteen minutes, she mused.

She looked every inch a capable adult, she decided. Her black hair grew in a pronounced widow's peak and was pushed back over her shoulders. The gentian blue of her eyes appeared even deeper than usual. The illumination of the kerosene lamp cast her bone structure into relief. Her high cheekbones stood out prominently. She thought she looked mysterious, glamorous, romantic. She watched as the smile of relief faded, leaving her full lips in a pout.

Now what should she do till Anna came? She'd light a dozen candles. When Anna arrived, they could have a drink by candlelight, and her aunt could tell her all about the autograph signing. Interesting things always happened to Anna. Susan glanced at her watch— eight-thirty. Only half an hour to wait.

When she was halfway to the kitchen to look for candle holders, she heard knocking at the front door. Anna was early! Susan picked up the kerosene lamp

and hurried to let her aunt in. She drew the bolt and
threw the door open. In the shadows a large man
huddled. His shoulders, hunched against the wind,
looked a yard wide. The wind whipped a shock of
black hair across his forehead. A scowl pulled his
brows together, and his eyes were a menacing black
glitter in the paleness of his face. Susan stood trans-
fixed in terror.

"Mind if I come in? It's starting to rain," he said in
a deep voice, and stepped in before she had the sense
to slam the door in his face.

"How did you get here?" she gasped.

"I walked."

"This is an island!"

His brows lifted. "You noticed. I see you're out of
power here, too."

Susan wanted to demand that he leave at once but
was afraid to confront him. "Who are you?" she
asked, her voice high with fear.

A closer look at her caller did nothing to lessen her
fear. In the lamplight, she saw that his complexion was
actually swarthy. With deep-set dark eyes he examined her closely, angrily. What right did he have to be
angry? she thought. *He* was the intruder! Susan hesitated to point that out to this man, who had shoulders as wide as a proverbial door. A fleecy navy shirt
stretched loosely across his wide chest. His close-
fitting jeans were spattered with raindrops, and his
sneakers were muddy. She knew he wouldn't have
stepped in mud coming up the flagstone path, so he
wasn't a stranded boater. Who was he, then?

Susan's lamp was shaking, and she put her other
hand on it to steady it.

"I'm your neighbor. Ogilvy's the name. Dan Ogilvy."

But surely the white cottage was empty! she thought. There was no boat at the dock.

"I was wondering if you could tell me where the generator is. I understand the island has its own generator."

"I have no idea. I just got here today myself," she said.

"Are you alone?"

To Susan the question sounded overwhelmingly ominous. Why did he want to know that? "No!" she said. It came out in a shout. "I'm with my aunt. She's—she's gone to bed." She added hastily, "But she's not asleep."

"Then maybe you'd ask her where the generator is. I might be able to get it started."

"Oh." Susan thought that this explanation, though reasonable, was still unsatisfactory. How did he plan to fix a generator in the dark? While she stood there, the man studied her questioningly. His dark eyes looked perfectly deadly. He just wanted to find out if she was really alone, she decided.

"Well?" He spoke arrogantly, impatiently.

Susan had no intention of going upstairs. What was to stop him from following her? Scenes from *Psycho* flashed through her mind. "My aunt doesn't know," she said stiffly. "Maybe Jed McClean could tell you. He's the handyman. I could phone him."

"How?" The word cut the air like a knife—swift, menacing. "There's no phone service on the island." The statement brought vividly to mind the fact that she was isolated with this stranger, cut off from the world.

The assessing glitter in his eyes emphasized it. He peered around the hallway. "You don't have a phone," he said accusingly. She was lying! he thought. Why?

Fear made Susan's voice tremble. "We have a cellular phone."

"Isn't that rather unusual?" Now, why the hell did two vacationing women need a cellular phone? he wondered. They cost a fortune, for one thing. Dillinger had objected to getting him one. And it wasn't arranged in a day, either. They weren't just vacationers, then. He'd better see what he could find out.

"Not in a place like this," she was saying. "How else could we keep in touch with—with people?" But she couldn't use the phone to get in touch with anyone unless this frightening man let her, she thought. Jed! She'd have to send a message to Jed to come at once. And that meant she had to get away from this man—Ogilvy—to make the call. "I'll phone Jed," she said.

"Where is this cellular phone?"

He was going to go into the study with her, unless she could divert him somehow. "In the office. Why don't you go into the living room and make yourself comfortable, Mr. Ogilvy? This won't take a minute."

"I'd like to see that phone, if you don't mind."

She knew he wasn't really asking permission. That arrogant face was saying he meant to watch her make the call and to listen. Or maybe it said something else. Maybe he just wanted to find the phone to put it out of commission so she would be totally cut off.

"You just dial, like an ordinary phone," she replied.

"Where is the office?" he asked. He stared at her, waiting.

Susan couldn't think of any other delaying tactics. "It's right in here."

Ogilvy stopped at the door and made a careful study of the room. Typewriter, bookshelves, bond paper. Nothing incriminating would be left on display, of course. But she'd been reluctant to let him into this room. Maybe the desk ... He strolled nonchalantly toward it.

Seeing that he was preoccupied, though she couldn't imagine why Anna's desk interested him, Susan walked silently and swiftly to the phone. Ogilvy turned at once and followed her. He stood immediately at her elbow, making her nervous.

"I have the number written right there, on that pad."

He glanced at it. A local number—that seemed all right. He handed it to her.

Susan set down the lamp and made the call, trying to steady her trembling fingers. How could she tell Jed she needed help, when Ogilvy was right beside her? "Hello, Mr. McClean?" she asked.

When Jed answered, she realized there was another problem. His voice came through loud and clear, and she was afraid Dan Ogilvy could hear his voice. "Did your aunt get there yet?" Jed asked.

Susan turned her back to her visitor. "Yes," she said, and asked about the generator.

"Why, Miss Milton knows where it is. Right in the middle of the island, halfway between the two cottages. How could she have forgotten that?"

"I don't know. Thanks, Mr. McClean." She peered over her shoulder. Ogilvy had returned to the desk. What was he looking for?

"Was there anything else?" Jed asked.

Susan's throat felt dry. "Yes," she said in a low tone.

Before she could say more, Ogilvy said, "I'd like to have a word with him," and came pouncing over. Panic washed over her. If Ogilvy spoke to Jed, he'd find out Anna wasn't here at all. She hung up the phone abruptly.

"Sorry. I'd already hung up," she said. And she hadn't gotten the message through to Jed. "It seems the generator's in the middle of the island. Do you know how to fix it?"

He studied her silently. The hell she had! She hung up *after* he asked to speak to that Jed. "That's what I planned to ask your handyman. First I'll have to find out what's wrong with it. I might not be able to do anything till morning."

She was lying! he marveled. What was it she didn't want him to know? It was strange that the aunt had gone to bed so early. The aunt must not be here at all. This woman probably didn't even know Anna Milton. What was she doing here? Who was she? Had someone discovered what he was doing on the island? Dillinger had taken every precaution. Ogilvy's mind roiled with questions, but he couldn't let her see his suspicions.

He consciously altered his voice to a friendly tone. "We might be in the dark till morning. At least you have oil lamps here."

Good lord, he was hinting that he was going to stay!
"I can lend you one," she offered at once.

Dan smiled carelessly, and when he spoke his tone
had an air of bantering flirtation. "Why, I'm beginning to get the feeling you're trying to be rid of me,
Miss—I don't believe I caught your name."

"Knight."

"Do you have a first name, or don't you believe in
using it on first acquaintance?"

"It's Susan." She was confused by the quick change
from menace to something very much like flirtation.
Had she let her imagination run riot? The man, Dan
Ogilvy, hadn't actually done anything except scare her
by his arrival. It *was* rather unusual to have a cellular
phone. Maybe he'd just wanted to see one, though
he'd showed more interest in the desk than the phone.
He hadn't tried to stop her from talking to Jed. She
could have cried "help" if she'd wanted to. She'd been
in a state of jitters before he arrived, and she'd pro-
jected her foolish fears onto him. As her terror subsided to fear, she began to assess Dan Ogilvy more
objectively.

"You can call Jed back, if you like," she said.

"If it doesn't need parts, I can fix it. If it does, Jed
isn't likely to have them. It'll have to wait till morning."

Susan went on examining him. She wouldn't call
him handsome exactly. His face was weathered, but it
was his eyes she found herself staring at. Alert, probing, intelligent eyes. In his rough shirt and jeans he
looked rugged, but that lean, athletic physique could
look elegant in the right clothes, she mused.

"I believe a Miss Milton owns the cottage," Dan said.

"That's right. Anna Milton's my aunt."

"Not *the* Anna Milton!" He didn't have to feign surprise. He'd known the owner's name was Milton, but no one had told him his neighbor would be the celebrated mystery writer. In fact, no one had told him Miss Milton would be in residence at all. She hardly ever came to the island, according to his sources. That was all he needed—a mystery buff snooping around!

"Yes, the Mistress of Mayhem," Susan said, using the title critics had conferred on her aunt.

"Will she be staying long?"

"For the summer, for a little rest. How long are you staying, Mr. Ogilvy?" People were usually happily surprised to learn Anna Milton was in their midst. Why had the news caused Mr. Ogilvy to frown?

"The same," he said, and attempted a smile, as though he were looking forward to the company.

"I'm surprised you can take so much time off from your job."

"Professors get the summers off. I'm here for the rest and relaxation, like you and your aunt."

Susan's feeling of danger had begun to fade. When the lights suddenly went on, the last trace of her nervousness vanished.

"Well!" she said, laughing in relief. "It seems you won't have to go charging through the bush in the dark after all. I wonder how the generator got back on. It's not as though we were on city hydro."

"It must be an intermittent problem," he said vaguely. Dan was wary once more. This woman was too damned bright! Obviously Golosov had found the generator and repaired it.

Susan checked her watch. It was nearly nine o'clock. She knew her aunt would soon be arriving, and since she'd told Dan Anna was in bed, she didn't want him to be here when her aunt came in. She was sorry to have to try to get him to leave just when he'd stopped being a menace. In fact, she wouldn't have minded offering him a drink. They were going to be neighbors, after all, and her first taste of isolation had shown her how welcome company would be. Dan Ogilvy would be a very nice relief from their lonesomeness. "I suppose you'll want to be getting back to your cottage before the rain breaks in earnest," she said with a friendly smile.

Dan's smile went a little beyond friendliness. He let his gaze play over Susan's face with no attempt at hiding his admiration. He liked classical looks. He didn't often see jet-black hair and those deep blue, almost indigo eyes. It was a bewitching combination.

"No hurry," he said. "I'm not afraid of a little rain. I'm all alone over there. Your aunt's in bed. . . ."

To Susan his implication was obvious—why don't you invite me to stay a while, maybe have a drink? She watched as he noticed the cocktail tray, set out and ready for Anna's arrival. Everything was there, including two unused glasses.

He asked, "Or are you expecting company?"

"No. It's been rather a long day. We came from New York this morning."

Dan's eyebrows rose, and his rumbling laugh was very natural. "It's not even nine o'clock!" he exclaimed.

"It's five to."

"But midnight is the witching hour, when princesses have to leave the party. A Knight should be more chivalrous. That's a pun, Miss Knight. The lowest form of humor. There—I beat you to it!"

"I like puns!" she objected.

"Then we have something in common. Did you hear the one about the bald hunter? A lousy shot. He lost his hare."

Dan had a warmly engaging smile. His eyes crinkled up at the corners, and his teeth were a flash of white in his weathered face. Susan felt herself smile instinctively in response to him. She was very reluctant to have him leave, but she was even more loath to have Anna walk in the door and make a liar of her.

"I don't want to give princesses a bad name, but I was up at six," she explained.

"I'm sorry. That was thoughtless of me. I wasn't even invited, and here I'm overstaying my wel—er, nonwelcome."

"It's not that! I'd—like to see you again."

"And so you shall, Miss Susan Knight."

Dan gave a mock-serious formal bow and turned to leave. He was just entering the hall when the front door burst open and Anna came flying in.

"What a night! I'm glad I made it across the river. It's starting to rain. Oh, Susan! You have company. How nice. I was worried about you, here all alone."

Dan turned his head slowly from one to the other. His surprise changed to amusement as he figured out the connection. Anna's face was familiar from the back cover of many books. "You must be Anna Milton," he said, his voice buzzing with suppressed laughter. "Your niece has just been telling me stories about you."

"Lies. All lies." Anna laughed and, putting her hand on Dan's elbow, led him off to the study.

Dan shot a mocking look over his shoulder at Susan. "I had already begun to suspect it," he said with a charming smile.

Chapter Two

As soon as the introductions were made, Anna said, "Is there anything to drink, Susan? My throat's parched. You'll stay for a drink, I hope, Mr. Ogilvy."

"I don't want to keep you ladies up. You've had a hard day's travel."

"Don't be absurd. It's not even nine o'clock," Anna said, laughing. "We never retire before midnight."

Anna's appearance confirmed that her grueling day hadn't fatigued her, Susan reflected. Her aunt's green eyes were as bright as stars. She was fifty but could easily be mistaken for ten years younger. She was a slight, wiry woman and had more energy than a squirrel.

Susan knew that when her aunt was at home working Anna looked like a shopping bag lady, but when she made public appearances she dressed to please her fans. For the Potsdam signing she'd chosen a cream designer suit and green accessories. Even in its wrinkled state from travel, it looked impressive, Susan thought. Anna's brick-colored hair had been lightened to a more stylish strawberry blond, worn short and brushed back from her forehead. Her face was fully made up, with extravagant eye shadow that photographed well but looked overdone to a live audience.

"Susan, would you do the honors?" Anna asked. "I'll have the usual. And you, Mr. Ogilvy—what would you like?"

The triumphant look in Dan's eyes when he smiled at Susan suggested that he'd already gotten what he wanted.

"Scotch'll be fine," he said.

Susan's trip to the kitchen for ice was a welcome escape. What on earth must Dan think of her? Yet she wasn't reluctant to return. Now that the fear had subsided, she was eager to see more of this Dan Ogilvy. When she returned, her aunt was gracefully acknowledging compliments on her reputation.

Anna turned to accept her drink, saying with a knowing look, "It's odd neither of you has mentioned the power failure." There was a suggestion in her glinting eye that romance was what had put it out of their minds, Susan thought. Anna was an incurable romantic.

"You're still leaving me in the dark, as it were, if you'll pardon an insignificant pun," she quipped.

"You're among friends—punsters all," Dan said, exchanging a brief look with Susan. "The power failure's the reason I'm here, actually."

He sat on the sofa with Anna. Susan took the chair beside it and studied Dan surreptitiously while her aunt engaged him in conversation. Why had she been afraid of him? He looked perfectly harmless now. His eyes, which had looked dangerously black, were actually a deep warm brown. His rugged face, seen in this new atmosphere, was no menace to anything, except possibly her peace of mind. It was a good, strong, masculine face. His nose was straight, and his jaw was a solid wedge.

"Mr. Ogilvy came to inquire about the generator," Susan explained. She continued to study him. She decided she could really become interested in a man like this—one who was mature and had a sense of humor. She hadn't felt at home with the men she'd met at college. Bookish and rather retiring, she'd felt ill at ease with those callow youths, who had seemed interested more in football than in anything else.

"I don't know what could have happened to it." Anna frowned. "There wasn't any lightning to knock it out of kilter. I'll have Jed McClean over to take a look at it in the morning. You're staying at Quinns' cottage, are you, Dan?"

"Yes, just down the beach from yours. It's the only other cottage on the island, I believe."

"That's right." Anna gave him a curious look. "How did you come to hear about it?"

Susan winced in embarrassment. Her aunt was going to go into one of her inquisitions, and Dan Ogilvy didn't look like a man who would sit still for much interrogation. He answered the question mildly enough, though.

"I saw an ad in the newspaper. I was looking for a quiet spot to rest and do some research, and an island just suited my needs, so I rented the place from the Quinns."

"I see." Anna nodded as though satisfied, but Susan caught a glitter of curiosity in her aunt's eyes. "I didn't realize the Quinns were renting. But then I haven't seen them since two summers ago. I didn't get here at all last year. And what is your particular field of research, Dan?"

"I'm a scientist."

"Interesting!" Anna's face beamed in approval.

Susan could easily interpret her aunt's thoughts. A scientist might prove extremely useful in providing clever and hard-to-detect means of murder.

"I'll be picking your brains over the summer. What a ghoulish expression—I love it!" Anna laughed.

"Mr. Ogilvy's a professor," Susan added.

"Then I expect we should be calling you Dr. Ogilvy," Anna said. "Which university, Doctor?"

"Massachusetts Institute of Technology. And I'd prefer you call me Dan."

"M.I.T. Very impressive! I would have thought a cottage in the Boston area would be more convenient." Anna's tone made it a question.

"I wanted to get away from the usual work environment."

Anna nodded. "I know just what you mean. I'm here for the same reason. Peace and quiet. I bought this retreat twenty years ago and so seldom get to use it that it's hardly worth keeping. And what is your special area of scientific interest at M.I.T., Dan?"

"I'm doing some research on artificial intelligence. Cybernetics, robotics," he said vaguely, thinking, that should stop her questions.

"Oh, robots! And is your family with you?"

"No, I came alone."

"I daresay a wife and children would be a distraction."

Susan waited with interest for Dan's answer. She hadn't thought of that! Dan intercepted her glance. She read the amusement he was trying to conceal and averted her eyes. But it was at Susan that he looked when he replied.

"I'm not married," Dan replied. "Or engaged," he added just as Anna appeared to be forming a discreet question to clarify it.

"I see." Anna smiled triumphantly. "Just we three foot-loose adults, alone on the island. You must feel free to drop in on us any evening you're lonesome."

"That's very kind of you. I'd return the offer, but I'm afraid I don't run a very elegant household. We bachelors, you know...."

"No need to apologize for a little clutter," Anna assured him. "That's half the charm of cottage life. I'm interested in hearing more about your research sometime. I'm always looking for a new topic to write about. I haven't done anything with a technical background."

"My research wouldn't be very interesting to the layman. It's pretty technical."

Susan saw his reluctance and was embarrassed when her aunt persisted.

"Oh, it would only be a background," Anna told him. "Naturally I wouldn't undertake to write a whole

book about science. I write about the human character. The devious twists and turns of the mind and the
heart that lead man to violate his instincts and take the
life of his fellowman. We're the only species that
murders, except animals killing one another to eat. In
a word, Dan, I write about murder." She added with
joyful relish, "Murder most foul."

Dan looked at his glass, then smiled playfully at
Anna. "Are you sure it's safe to drink this?" he asked.

She laughed merrily. "I have no reason to murder
you—yet," she quipped, wagging a playful finger.

"It's your niece who prepared the drink." Dan
turned to Susan, using it as an excuse to lure her into
the conversation. "Poison is a lady's method of doing
away with the unwanted, I believe."

Again it was Anna who answered. "Women are using guns more, now that they're so easily available,"
she said, and went on with some statistics.

Susan was aware that while her aunt talked, Dan's
dark eyes often strayed to Susan. It seemed every time
she glanced up, he was studying her. She didn't think
it was Anna's statistics of violent death that caused
that smile and the glow in his eyes.

Anna soon rose. "I'm going upstairs to unpack,
Dan. You and Susan have another drink. It was a
pleasure to meet you. I hope we see a good deal of you
this summer."

Dan rose and shook her hand. "It was an honor to
meet you, Miss Milton. I confess I haven't read any of
your books yet, but now that I've met you, I look
forward to the pleasure."

"You'll find copies of some of my books on the top
shelf. I recommend *Abra Cadaver*. And by the way,

my friends call me Anna." Then she smiled graciously and left.

As soon as she was gone, Dan turned a questioning look to Susan. "I don't claim to be an Adonis, but did I really look that frightening?"

She didn't have to ask what he meant. Why had she told him her aunt was upstairs? Now that she knew him a little, her charade did seem childish. The man she was looking at was obviously civilized, educated, intelligent, handsome—and presumably law-abiding.

"To tell the truth, I just got a case of the jitters when I was alone here and the lights went out."

"What did you think I was going to do, murder you? I'll blame it on your aunt's influence. I know Anna's a mystery writer, but what do you do, Susan?"

"I'm her secretary." Till she had a book accepted, Susan wouldn't announce to the world that she was trying to write one.

Dan idly swished the ice around in his glass. "Anna mentioned another drink. It's still a couple of hours from midnight, and your wicked stepaunt has left."

"You've got the roles mixed up!" Susan objected. "Anna's been more like a fairy godmother to me."

While Susan prepared the drink, Dan began a series of questions that sounded like ordinary conversation but were in fact designed to discover as much as he could about Susan Knight. She answered so easily and unhesitatingly that he knew she was either telling the truth or had been well coached. Her deference to Anna seemed to indicate that she really was a less privileged niece of the celebrated writer. The change in life-style would account for that air of uncertainty of Susan's that charmed him. Her new position certainly hadn't gone to her head.

"From Philadelphia to the life-style of the rich and famous—quite a jump," he remarked.

"I still can't believe it."

Satisfied with the interrogation, Dan went to the bookshelves. He brought *Abra Cadaver* to the table, where Susan was just giving his fresh drink a stir. The candles and kerosene lamp were still burning. As she bent over the glass, Dan admired the sweep of her long lashes and the accentuated widow's peak. The graceful movement of her hands reminded him of a ballerina's.

He wished he could have met Susan at some other time, in some other place. There was an air of old-world charm about her that enchanted him. The contrast of ivory skin and ebony hair suggested a Victorian cameo. She looked like a woman who would know how to blush. Her charm went beyond mere physical beauty. She was gentle spoken, a little shy, but not gauchely backward. Away from her aunt she was more talkative. She reminded him of a violet, blooming in the shade of the more exotic Anna Milton. Once in a rare while, two people met and felt at once that they were made for each other. That was the way he felt about Susan Knight, and the timing could hardly be worse.

Susan looked up and handed him the drink, and he found himself gazing into the dark gentian pools of her eyes, mesmerized.

"It's not poison, if taken in moderation," she said, and smiled.

Good-humored, too, he mused. It really was a shame he'd have to get rid of her. One thing was certain; he couldn't have a mystery writer rooting out his secrets on the island this summer. Project ISE was already a confidential matter, even without the added problem of Golosov.

"A toast, to murder most foul," he said, and drank.

"You'll get used to Anna's conversation," she replied, and began blowing out the candles and lamp.

Dan watched silently as she puckered her lips for the job. It made her full, ripe mouth nearly irresistible. in fact, his reaction was so strong that he reached out and extinguished the last two candles between his fingers.

"Show-off," Susan said, and sat on the sofa. Dan sat beside her.

"Isn't it going to be hard for you, doing your research here?" she asked. "I thought you'd need access to the Institute's library and probably to other experts in the field."

"It's true no scientist works in a vacuum. We all stand on the shoulders of past giants, but this summer I'll be doing some preliminary theoretical work. That I can do alone."

"I must confess I didn't clearly understand what you said about your work, but doesn't artificial intelligence involve computers?"

Dan had no intention of discussing his work and adroitly changed the subject. "This research is just a long-term thing I do during my summers. We can find something more interesting to talk about."

"Long-term?" she asked, frowning. "I thought the computer business was so competitive everything was done on the double. The Japanese will beat you to whatever you're doing if you only do it in the summers."

Dan felt a flash of alarm. He was really going to have to be careful with these women; they were too sharp. "You're probably right. I should get the lead out. My real job is teaching. I'm just doing some rather complicated mathematical work to help out a colleague."

He talked about some of his classes. Susan got a hazy impression that mathematics was his true love. She'd let Anna do her own digging to see if there was a book in it. Susan enjoyed just having some pleasant, masculine company, more or less her own age. Dan didn't look older than thirty. Susan was twenty-four, so most of Anna's friends and colleagues were too old for her. She didn't really mind. Marriage wasn't a part of her immediate plans.

She meant to be a career writer, like Anna. Susan had often mentally compared her mother's life to Anna's. Marriage meant settling down in the suburbs and taking care of a husband and family. It meant cooking and cleaning. One couldn't combine a full-time career with so many other duties. She'd have only a few hours in the evening for her work.

A successful author, on the other hand, was her own boss. Anna went on trips to Europe and all over. Susan and her aunt had just gotten back from a delightful month in England. Anna was asked to give speeches at universities and at writers' conventions. She had a wide network of friends in all walks of life. Her research led to her making friends in the universities, the police department, politics, medicine and, of course, literature. It was a full, rewarding life.

And if one loved writing as much as Anna and Susan did, it was fun, too.

But still, she found it interesting to meet someone like Dan. Susan wasn't so single-minded that she ruled out romance entirely. In fact, Dan would be the perfect man for her first serious fling. They'd have two months together, and when the summer was over, they'd go their separate ways. And maybe, just maybe, she'd have learned something about love.

What would it be like to kiss Dan? A shadow of incipient whiskers around his jaw emphasized his masculinity. His lips were carved with the sensuous fullness of a Grecian statue. Praxiteles's Hermes in the British Museum had lips like that, only the statue's lips were cold stone, she thought languorously. Dan's were warm flesh and blood.

Dan watched her. She hadn't spoken for two minutes. Was she even listening to him? That story about the thirteen-year-old student with an IQ of two hundred usually got some reaction. Susan looked as if she were miles away. What was going on behind those dreamy indigo eyes? She was probably just tired.

He set his glass down. The sound stirred her back to attention. "Thanks for the drink. It's time for me to be going now."

"Oh, are you leaving so soon?" she asked, startled.

"I'm afraid I'm keeping you awake—almost."

He noticed a flush stained her cheeks.

"I'm sorry. I am a little tired," she said. Now, why was he smiling like that, so smugly? she wondered. "What did I say?"

"It's not what you said; it's the way you said it—with a blush. And I haven't even told you how beautiful you are."

She felt her color deepen as his gaze lingered on her face, moving from eyes to nose to lips.

"You are, you know."

As he continued staring, Susan felt her first surge of pleasure turn to embarrassment. She had never been scrutinized so closely before and found herself answering curtly. "Beauty lies in the eye of the beholder."

"This beholder likes what he beholds." He continued to study her for a long, disconcerting moment. "And now I'll really leave, before the dread word flattery rears its head."

She rose to accompany him to the door, feeling awkward and ill at ease. She had handled that simple compliment abominably, she mused. The weather made a welcome diversion. The wind was still high, but the heavy rain held off.

"Better batten down the hatches. It looks like we're in for a storm," Dan said.

The river was covered with whitecaps, and the tree branches whipped violently overhead. "You'd better hurry. Good night, Dan," she said softly.

A smile curved his lips. What would she say if he pulled her into his arms and kissed her till her toes curled? he wondered. He just touched her chin lightly with his index finger. "See you tomorrow, Susan." He waved goodbye and went out into the blackness.

Susan watched as he jogged along the beach to his cottage. She really botched that leave-taking. He must know already, after only one visit, that she was un-

comfortable with a man. Dan was entirely different
from anyone she'd ever dated. He was older, more intelligent and much more attractive. She usually became bored with men after two or three dates. She had
a strong feeling that Dan would grow more interesting on longer acquaintance.

It was strange, she thought, that he'd gone home by
the beach, but he must have come by one of those
paths through the bush. She recalled that his shoes had
been muddied. He'd just arrived on the island, so how
had he found his way in the dark? The coast was the
easier path, and the pebble beach was wide enough
that he could negotiate it without wetting his shoes.

She remembered the noise she'd heard outside the
office earlier. Was it possible Dan had been peeking in
through the window? She'd seen something move
outside and thought it was just the bushes. No, Dan
wouldn't do something like that. He seemed very nice.
But in the morning she'd check outside the window for
footprints.

Susan didn't mention any of this when Anna came
into her bedroom later. It was the sort of thing her
aunt would latch on to and embroider into a whole
intrigue. Two summers ago Anna had reported one of
the local islanders as a dope pusher and white-slave
trader because while she'd been picknicking on one of
the public islands she'd seen Dr. Buell giving an injec-
tion to a young woman. It had turned out the girl was
his daughter and he was giving her an insulin shot for
her diabetes.

Anna had changed into a comfortable terry house-
coat. Her face was shining from its nightly lathering
of cream. She rubbed the excess into her hands.

"Darned liver spots," she complained. "The French call them flowers of death—isn't that gruesome?"

"You're gruesome." Susan smiled.

"I do my best. I like your Dan Ogilvy, by the way. The summer might be more interesting than we thought."

"We're here to work, too, Anna," Susan replied. The specific work she had in mind was finishing her own novel.

"We might have our work cut out for us. You know, I suppose, that Dan wasn't telling us the truth."

"I thought I noticed your 'mystery' expression while you were talking to Dan." Susan was curious to hear what new plot her aunt had come up with. "What do you mean?"

"He didn't rent that cottage from the Quinns. I phoned them before we left New York to see if they'd be here. They've sold it."

"Maybe Dan bought it."

"He said he rented it. Besides, it was sold to a company, not an individual. I expect I'll get an offer for my place any day now. The company must want the whole island I should think. Dan's just plain trespassing. Now, isn't that interesting?" Anna mused.

"Maybe he rented the cottage for the summer— from the company, I mean."

Anna shook her head sagely. "No, he said he'd rented it from the Quinns. The only possibility is that the deal fell through and the Quinns decided to rent. I'll give Nora Quinn a call tomorrow and find out."

"Why would he make up such a story?" Susan asked.

"I can think of any number of reasons," the ever-inventive Anna replied. "He could be hiding out from the law or from a wife after alimony. Or he could be a plain cheapskate, a squatter using the cottage rent free."

"A professor wouldn't be that poor."

"Professor?" Anna asked, and laughed. "Yes, if he *is* a professor. I never met one before who didn't bore my ears off with a lecture on his work at the first hint of interest. Dan, you noticed, closed up like an oyster.

"And another thing," Anna added blandly, "he said he was alone there. He isn't. I saw a man outside the cottage as I drove past. He had a flashlight, or I'd never have spotted him. He put it out as soon as he saw the boat, but there was another man there, all right. And you noticed how when I intimated to Dan that we'd drop in on him he tried to keep us away with that silly story of the place being cluttered."

Susan listened with interest to all this. She remembered Dan's menacing look when he'd first barged into the cottage. He'd behaved dangerously enough till she'd told him she wasn't alone. Her disbelief began to fade away.

"I think he was peeking in the windows, too," she admitted, and told her aunt about Dan's muddied shoes. "And it was certainly strange that the generator went back on of its own accord."

"Strange? It's impossible."

They discussed the whys and wherefores of these mysteries for a few minutes.

"What do you think we should do?" Susan asked.

"Nothing to curtail our summer's entertainment, if it's reporting him to the police you have in mind."

"We don't want to be alone on the island with two men who could be dangerous. It was really scary before you came, Anna. Maybe one of them's an escaped convict or something. They could kill us," Susan pointed out.

"Jed would have warned ut of any escaped convicts in the area. I hardly think murder is what they have in mind. Perhaps they plan to kidnap me. I've never been kidnapped. It should be very interesting," Anna said calmly. But she reached into her bedside table and drew out a pearl-handled pistol, which she put under her pillow.

"That's fine for you, Anna, but I don't have a gun."

"If kidnapping's their game, it *could* be you they're after, planning to get the money from me. What a sensation it would make if they should succeed! We'd be on the front page of every paper in the country. And there'd certainly be an excellent book in it afterward."

"If there is an afterward! Kidnappers have been known to kill their victims," Susan pointed out.

"Oh, Dan didn't look like a murderer to me. I'll make a few phone calls tomorrow and see if I can find out just who he is, exactly. If he's really from M.I.T., my friends there will know him."

"And if he isn't?"

"Then we'll have to get a picture of him and the other man and have the FBI run them for us. Fingerprints, too. I'll get those at dinner tomorrow night. We shall invite Dr. Ogilvy to dinner."

"We already have his fingerprints on a glass down-stairs."

"You're right! Run down and bring it up immedi-ately, Susan. We don't want Nell washing it. She might be here before we're up in the morning."

Though Susan knew her aunt was an alarmist, kid-napping *was* possible. Why take chances? "Maybe we should leave the island till this thing is settled," she suggested.

Anna shook her head firmly. "If you have any in-tention of becoming a mystery writer, Susan, you must seize every opportunity that comes along. The fact is, premeditated murder it quite rare. Murder most often occurs accidentally due to a fit of passion, usually within a family. Occasionally it's done for financial gain. We'll sit tight, keep the pistol loaded and handy and keep a sharp eye on Dan Ogilvy—or whoever he is."

Susan got Dan's glass and she and Anna went to bed. It wasn't until she was under the covers that she had time to reconsider the matter more objectively. Why did she always fall for Anna's crazy ideas? Anna's imagination was legendary. She could find a mystery in a broken shoelace or a cigarette butt. To-night she'd found a "kidnapper" in a harmless cot-tage tenant. Dan might have rented the cottage for the summer before the Quinns had sold it. If the com-pany that bought it had had no immediate plans for the island, he might have been allowed to stay for the summer.

As for the other man with the flashlight, it could have been anyone. The water on the river was becom-ing rough, and a boater might have stopped for safety's sake. For that matter, Anna had complained more than once about people using the island for picnics and wiener roasts. But meanwhile Anna's imagination would ensure that Dan was often in their company, and Susan looked forward to that.

She lay awake a long time, reliving in her mind the drive from New York, the arrival at the island, the scare of the lights going out and Dan's arrival. They were all jumbled together in her head, flashing images like a movie collage. And at the back of her mind she thought of Dan saying she was beautiful. He was the beautiful one—well, handsome.

Just as she was drifting off to sleep, she thought of Dan's sneakers, which had been caked with mud around the bottom though he'd gone home by the beach, where there *was* no mud.

At the Quinns' cottage, Zinovi Golosov was waiting for Dan Ogilvy. Golosov's wool suit was heavy for June, and its cut was vaguely foreign. His broad, Slavic face wore a wary look.

"Sorry I was gone so long," Dan said. "I had to find out a few things. The Milton woman and her niece plan to spend the summer at the cottage. We'll have to get rid of them. Project ISE isn't exactly public information, and you, Zin, are definitely top secret. What was the matter with the generator?"

Golosov understood English better than he spoke it. His reply sounded like "filter," so Dan assumed the filter had been clogged. Golosov must have replaced it. Dan frowned. "The woman at the cottage thought it was strange the generator started up by itself. I wish Dillinger had found a safe place for you. We didn't

have much time, of course, and I do welcome the opportunity for you to have a look at Project ISE.''

Golosov nodded, and Dan continued. ''Windmill
Island was owned by two influential families who like
their privacy, and people have learned over the years
that they aren't welcome here. Taking the project into
account, we thought this seemed like a good choice.
Dillinger checked it out. He said the Milton woman
practically never comes. Too bad she chose this year
to be different. The company will have to make her an
offer, and she'd better accept it.''

Dan knew there was no point worrying Golosov, but
what if Anna didn't accept the offer? How could he
get rid of her? They'd just have to make her an offer
she couldn't refuse. She had mentioned she doesn't get
much use from the place, so she would probably sell.
''Have you checked my figures on the angle of installation for the panels?'' he asked. Golosov nodded.

''Good, then the motor will turn the panels to follow the sun. We can begin the installation soon.''
Dan's frown eased. ''We'll wait a few days till the ladies are gone. There's still paperwork to do.''

Golosov narrowed his eyes and smiled. Dan continued. ''It'll only be for a few days, and we'll have
plenty to do. And now how would you like a hotdog
and cola before we hit the sack?'' Golosov gave a wide
smile. Zin was becoming a real Yank, Dan mused.
Tomorrow he'd get him some hamburgers.

''Oh, and one other thing, Zin,'' Dan added. ''The
women think I'm alone. You'll have to keep out of
sight till they're gone. Sorry about that.''

Golosov made a rumbling sound of displeasure, and Dan said, "You'll be thinking America's no better than Russia." The Russian's signs of displeasure vanished when Dan handed him a can of cola.

Chapter Three

The last sound Susan heard before she drifted off to sleep was the haunting echo of horns from ships passing in the channel. It was also the first sound she was aware of the next morning. Like a train whistle in the distance, it conjured up thoughts of faraway places. As the echo died away she heard birds chirping and smiled. Sunlight, as clear as crystal, poured through her open drapes. The sky looked as though it had never heard of smog; it was a dazzling blue. This was how the world was meant to be, she marveled, and hopped out of bed, eager to begin the day.

She pulled on a blue flannel shirt and jeans. The tantalizing aroma of freshly perked coffee and sizzling bacon wafting upstairs sharpened her appetite. She hastily twisted her black hair into one side braid and went downstairs.

The woman bustling about the kitchen looked the way Susan had pictured Jed McClean's wife. Nell was middle-aged and rather plain in appearance. Her brown hair was turning gray around the temples, and she wore an apron over her cotton dress.

"Good morning. I'm Susan Knight. You must be Mrs. McClean."

"Call me Nell. Are you ready for breakfast, Miss Knight?"

"I heard my aunt getting dressed. I'll wait and eat with her. I want to go outside for a moment."

"It's going to be a nice day," Nell prophesied.

Susan went outside into the chilly morning air. Toward the east the sky was puffed with white cotton clouds. The island's greenery, washed by the rain, shone as if it were brand-new. There couldn't possibly be anything illegal happening in a place like this, she thought, but decided to check outside the office window just to satisfy her curiosity. Or would the rain have wiped out any footprints?

She hurried to the east side of the cottage. The roof's overhang had kept the rain from splashing the ground much. The outlines of a man's footprints were etched clearly in the drying earth. The marks had been left by sneakers like those Dan had been wearing. Susan felt a shiver of revulsion. He had been out there last night, spying on her when she'd been alone.

The tracks led toward the back of the house, where an opening in the bush caught her attention. She followed the path, glancing around to make sure she was alone. Before long she came upon a small metal barn-like building in a clearing. The door was closed but not locked. The generator, obviously, she thought. She pushed the door open, and the stench of diesel oil assailed her. The motor was humming merrily.

As she peered into the dark windowless building, the only unusual item she saw was a metal cylinder resting on the floor. It was about eight inches long and had some kind of mechanism inside it. The oil oozing from it indicated that it had recently been removed from the motor. Was this the piece that had broken down last night? she wondered. She knew Dan hadn't replaced it; he'd been with her when the generator had started up again. A spurt of alarm sharpened her awareness. It must have been the man Anna had seen at Quinns' wharf. Susan carried the mechanism back to Sans Souci with her to show Jed. She hurried along the bush-edged path back to the house looking over her shoulder and scuttled into the safety of the kitchen. Nell looked at the piece from the generator.

"What's that you've got there, Miss Knight? It looks like the old oil filter from the generator. I guess Jed got the new one put in after all. It usually gets clogged up over the winter. There's no point saving the old one. With the diesels, when it gets dirty, you just replace it." She took it from Susan and put it outside.

But Jed hadn't been on the island last night...Susan thought, alarmed.

The walk in the fresh air had given her a sharp appetite. She washed her hands, then joined her aunt at the breakfast table. Anna sat sipping her coffee, wearing an old yellow sweater and woolen slacks. Susan told her about the footprints and the filter.

"Excellent," Anna said happily. Her chest swelled with importance, giving her the air of a pouter pigeon. "The plot thickens. You'll never guess what,

Susan. I called Ivor Mallen at M.I.T. They've never heard of Dr. Ogilvy there." This news, which troubled Susan, lent a glow of exultation to her aunt.

"Did you call the Quinns?" Susan asked.

"Indeed I did! That cellular phone is worth its weight in gold. Nora tells me her cottage was sold to a company called Sun Inc. Her husband is checking into it. It isn't on the New York stock exchange, nor the American. It must be a small outfit. In any case Dan Ogilvy is an outright fraud." Her smile made this accusation a compliment of the highest order.

"I wonder who he can be."

"I haven't the faintest idea, but I'll make it my business to find out. I'll wrap the glass with Dan's fingerprints on it and send it to that nice Mr. Scott, the very clever private investigator from Washington who helped me with my research for *Night Crossing*. He used to be with CIA and knows everyone. He even does work for the government, so he can weasel favors out of the police and the FBI. They'll run the prints for him. Oh, and I must buy film while I'm ashore."

Nell brought in plates of waffles and bacon. "This is real maple syrup," she announced, setting a glass jug on the table.

Anna patted her hips disparagingly. "I really shouldn't," she said, and poured a dollop of the syrup over her golden waffles. "We'll want to get a picture of Dan tonight when he comes to dinner."

"You're still asking him to dinner!" Susan exclaimed, incredulous.

"Absolutely! Right after breakfast I want you to run over to the Quinns' and invite him for tonight."

"He practically told us to stay away," Susan reminded her aunt.

"You have to develop a little thicker skin, my dear. What do you care what he thinks of you? It's just business. I've written him a note. Tell him it needs an answer, and he'll have to ask you in while he reads it. Keep your eyes open for any sign of the other man."

"It might be dangerous" was Susan's next objection.

"Not when I know you're there. If he intended any harm to us, he wouldn't do it at his own cottage. He'd attack us when we were alone, with no witness and no one to know where we were."

"How reassuring," Susan said, and finally took a bite of Nell's delicious breakfast.

While she ate and Anna gabbled, Susan tried to sort out fact from Anna's fiction. Apparently Dan wasn't just an ordinary professor on vacation. He wasn't who he said he was, but that didn't automatically make him a kidnapper or some kind of criminal. It was hardly likely he'd come to the island to harm them when they didn't even know him. She wasn't afraid to go to his cottage in broad daylight. Maybe he would explain those footprints outside the study window. There could be an innocent reason—he could have been running away from a skunk. And the other lies? Well, she'd reserve judgment. Innocent till proven guilty.

When they'd finished breakfast, Anna said, "I'll take a quick run over to the mainland. I must decide what to feed Dan tonight. Steak, do you think?"

Susan felt a wrench inside at the thought that she'd never get to know Dan well enough to learn these little intimate details. "You can't go far wrong with steak."

"Later I'll read your manuscript, Susan. I'm looking forward to it. *Old Lover's Ghost*. I like your title. From Shakespeare, of course."

"John Donne, actually."

"The same period of English literature," Anna said, to cover her error.

This was the day Susan had been waiting for. She respected Anna's opinion, and despite the real-life mystery that was brewing, she was on tenterhooks for Anna's opinion of her novel. By nightfall she would know whether the book she'd worked so hard on was any good. Susan was sure the whole thing would be thrown in the wastebasket. Her hero was made of wood, her heroine of marshmallow, and her plot was contrived and implausible.

Susan took her aunt's note for Dan and went outdoors. She headed automatically for the shore but decided to take one of the paths through the bush instead. It was easy for her to figure out which path to take. Of the three, two were overgrown, so she took the cleared one. The markings from Dan's running shoes were still visible in the drying mud, and she now knew he'd come to the cottage this way last night. It seemed he'd done so because he hadn't wanted to be seen by anyone passing in a boat. She followed the path and soon came out at the back door of the other cottage.

Another path led from the back of the cottage toward the center of the island. Susan saw that the long grass had been trodden down and knew someone had taken that path, too, then, probably to the generator.

Dan's kitchen light was on. She assumed he was having breakfast. She rapped and waited for a few moments. She thought he hadn't heard her. She tried the screen door outside the white frame one, but it was locked. She knocked again, more loudly. Still there was no answer. That was strange, she mused. She was about to knock again when she saw movement behind the curtains. Dan must have heard her now. But when he finally came out, he used the front door and called around to the back.

"Good morning," he shouted. "It looks like we're in for a nice day."

"It's a little chilly," Susan called as she walked to the front. After she'd spoken, she realized it sounded like a hint for him to invite her in.

"You're up bright and early," Dan remarked.

It was hard for her to read his expression. He was smiling, but the smile had a rigid look and didn't reach his eyes. As for the rest of him, he was even more attractive than she remembered. A fresh shave had removed the shadowy look from his lower face. In the bright sunlight his eyes glowed with health.

The pale blue fleecy shirt he wore today clung to his strong chest. The words Massachusetts Institute of Technology were printed in faded white across the front. Why would he have a well-worn M.I.T. shirt if he wasn't connected with the institution? On the other hand, why not? She'd bought one that said Oxford University when she was in England.

"I have a letter for you," she said, and handed it to him.

A look of alarm flashed across his face. "Have you been to the mainland for mail already?"

"No, it's from Anna. She'd like an answer." Her reply satisfied him. At least his look of alarm faded.

She rubbed her arms against the morning air, hoping he'd invite her in. Dan opened the envelope and scanned the note. Anna would have been offended at the way his brows drew together in a frown, Susan reflected. He was going to refuse, she thought, and was disappointed. She'd been looking forward to that dinner party.

Dan looked up questioningly. "It's an invitation to dinner."

"I know. I hope you can come."

Dan considered that for a moment. Susan wondered why a man who was all alone would have to stop to consider it. He should have been delighted. Anna wasn't exactly nobody; her invitations were sought after.

Dan stared at the invitation, thinking. He didn't want to leave Golosov alone again, but he knew it would look odd for him to refuse. It wouldn't be a good idea to excite Anna's curiosity too much. And Susan would be there....

"I'd be delighted to come," he said, smiling.

Susan noticed the corners of his eyes crinkled now— he'd smiled with genuine pleasure, or a good imitation—but he hadn't warmed up enough to invite her in for coffee. "Fine. I'll tell Anna to expect you."

"Will it be formal-ish?"

"Anna didn't say, but she likes to dress up. Did you bring a suit?"

"I did, and a tie. I'll be there at seven. I'll even polish my shoes."

That reminded Susan of the footprints. Glancing at Dan's shoes, she saw he was wearing moccasins today. She could think of no discreet way of asking him whether he'd been peeking in her window the night before.

"Well, I'll let you get back to work now," he said with enough heartiness that she knew he wanted to sound friendly but also wanted to get rid of her.

"Fine. I'll see you tonight."

"I'm looking forward to it."

She went home by the shore route and reported to Anna, who found it extremely suspicious that Dan hadn't opened the kitchen door or invited Susan in. Anna had the glass for Bill Scott wrapped and ready for mailing. Susan offered to take it for her so that her aunt could begin reading *Old Lover's Ghost*.

"Fine. Nell will show you how to operate the boat. Don't forget to buy film, Susan, and pick up any morning newspapers you can find. Since we were abroad we've been out of touch with what's been going on. There's an outside chance that Dan's an escaped convict," Anna said. "I hope he's something more interesting than an embezzler or tax dodger. What a letdown it would be if he's only a white-collar criminal."

Nell accompanied Susan to the boat house. The launch, an old but beautifully crafted Garwood with a sleek varnished wood body, gleamed where the sun struck it. "Take care of the *Stella Maris*," Nell said. "She's a collector's item, Miss Knight. They don't make them like this anymore."

"She's a beauty!"

"That's a nice boat the man next door's been driving, too," Nell said. "But newer, of course."

Susan's head jerked up in surprise. "*Been* driving? What do you mean? Has he been on the island long?"

"Just a few days, but he's made so many trips to Westburg that I couldn't help noticing, even though he always does his delivering after dark."

"What does he deliver?"

"It's hard to tell at night. The parcels are all wrapped up in heavy coverings like what furniture movers use. I suppose he's bringing furnishings over. That's odd, too, since the Quinns' place is fully furnished."

Susan's scalp tingled with interest. Dan Ogilvy got odder by the minute. "Did you ever see another man with him, Nell?"

"No, he's always alone. Since I live right close to the marina, I've seen him there often. He gets one of the marina hands to help him load the furniture, but I'll be darned if I know how he unloads it alone once he gets here. Jed thought he might get a little work out of him, but Mr. Ogilvy didn't seem interested. He's quite a loner. Never goes to the tavern in the evenings as you'd think he might, being all alone here."

This confirmed that someone had been visiting Dan. Susan decided to do a little investigating while she was ashore. Anna would do no less. "Where does he store all this furniture exactly?"

"At Bob Carney's Marina. But he's finished his delivering now. Last night was the last of it, or so Bob told Jed."

Obviously Anna wasn't the only one who was interested in Dan Ogilvy's doings. In a small community little passed unnoticed. Susan tried fishing for more information. "Did Bob Carney say it was furniture Ogilvy was delivering?"

"Bob doesn't know himself. The stuff all came in from New York, which is funny, since Ogilvy's license plate says Boston. The lot of it arrived in an unmarked van at night. All very secretive," Nell said pensively.

"Yes, isn't it? I know my aunt would appreciate it if you'd let her know anything else you hear about Mr. Ogilvy."

"She's having him to dinner. Why doesn't she ask him herself?"

Susan answered reluctantly. "Mr. Ogilvy doesn't always tell the truth, I'm afraid."

Nell shook her head in wonderment. "It sounds like one of Miss Milton's books."

"It will be, undoubtedly."

Nell went back into the cottage, and Susan turned on the boat's engine. She eased the boat out of the boat house and headed into the channel, opening the throttle. There were no large ships close enough to cause concern today. As she increased speed, the water sprayed up around her, and the boat left a wide swath of foam in its wake. She found that it was like flying, only more interesting because of the physical interaction with the elements. The wind pulled her hair out behind her, whistled in her ears and snatched at her shirt. A friendly fisherman raised his hand and smiled. He didn't seem to mind that she was probably disturbing the fish. Islands loomed up ahead, then slid by in a flash of green. The pines seemed to be waving at her in the wind. It was such a sunny, friendly place it seemed impossible that anything sinister could be going on.

Susan docked the launch at Bob Carney's Marina and ran up the hill into the town, if it could be called a town. Westburg was really just an overgrown village of three blocks long, but it did have a post office, where Susan mailed the package to Scott. Her next stop was the drugstore, where she could buy film and pick up the papers. Susan was a compulsive peruser of the paperback racks. While she pored over the mysteries, she noticed Dan pass down the next aisle. His head was bent, and he was frowning. She crouched to avoid being seen.

Dan went to the phone booth at the back of the store. She hid her face behind a book and peered around the edge of it. He took a long time putting money into the slot so she knew he wasn't making a local call. Why had he come to the mainland just to make a phone call? He could have asked Anna if he could use her phone. Unless he wanted complete privacy for his call, of course. . . .

Deciding it was her duty to follow Dan when he left, Susan grabbed her papers, got the film and paid the cashier, then went back to the book rack to wait till he finished his call. Before long he came out of the phone booth, smiling. He picked up a few things—potato chips, candy bars. With that lean, hard body, he didn't look as if he were a junk-food addict, Susan mused. A wistful smile pulled at her lips. She hadn't expected this boyish streak in him and found it rather endearing.

When Dan paid the cashier and left, Susan slipped out of the store a few steps behind him. She looked up and down, then across the street. She stared, open-mouthed. It was impossible, but he had vanished.

In the low-slung silver Mercedes parked across the road, Dan peered through the windows. Yes, she was looking for him, all right. Why? Anna Milton, being a celebrity, was on file and easy to verify. *She* was definitely who she'd said she was, but Susan Knight could be anyone.

He'd had a very bad moment when she'd handed him that letter. If she'd made inquiries at the post office she might have learned more than was comfortable. She might be an agent, billeted on Miss Milton for a cover. And if certain people had discovered Golosov was on the island, they would definitely have assigned an agent. He would have thought it would be a man, but a woman seemed less suspicious. Whatever, he'd know soon. The query he'd made should be answered today, since he'd learned where Miss Knight was *supposed* to have been born and educated. He was probably being overly cautious to have used a pay phone, but he couldn't take any chances of his phone being bugged on that particular call.

The half dozen letters Dan had picked up at the post office were on the seat beside him. He smiled in satisfaction at the "Dr. Ogilvy" on the envelope and threw them into the back seat. Dillinger was wide awake on that score, at least, he reflected.

When he saw Susan turn to walk away, he honked the horn. She turned around, and he lowered the window and called out, "Can I give you a lift?"

"Dan!" So that's where he'd gotten to so quickly, she thought as she walked toward the car, admiring its sleek lines. "Nice wheels!" She glanced at the license plate. Nell was right; the plates said Boston.

"I pampered myself. Why don't you hop in and let me show it off?"

"I'm just going to the dock."

"You can spare some time for a quick tour of the neighborhood. There should be some pretty scenery around here."

Susan was undecided. A part of her wanted to jump in beside Dan, but discretion held her back. She didn't really believe he wanted to harm her. On the other hand, she had no wish to repeat those moments of terror when she'd first been alone with him at Sans Souci. She remembered Anna's warning. If he meant to harm them, he'd do it when nobody knew where they were. Anna knew she'd gone to the mainland, but no one would know she'd accepted a ride with Dan, and she'd be at his mercy.

"It's such a nice day, I'd rather walk, thanks."

"I'll join you," Dan said. He rolled up the windows and got out. "Can I take your packages?"

She handed them to him, and he took a quick peek in the bag as he put them into the car. Film—that could be perfectly innocent, or she could have plans to make him and Golosov her models. He locked the car. "We'll stop for a coffee later. I owe you one. I should have asked you in this morning, but I didn't want you to see the dirty dishes in the sink." He decided to listen closely to her accent as she replied.

What else didn't you want me to see? Susan wondered. "I've seen dirty dishes before."

"Three days old?"

"Three days! Have you been here that long?"

"Four, actually. Why do you look so surprised?"

"I—I thought you just arrived last night."

"Oh, because I didn't know where the generator was. I hadn't explored the island's interior, but I had been along the coast. I confess I even did some window peeking at Anna's place, coveting Sans Souci. My intention was to try to hire it instead, if it was going to be empty." Dan noticed her avid interest in this and realized that she had seen the footprints. But her accent was perfect—though, of course, agents could come from Philadelphia.

"Anna never rents out her place." Susan was relieved to hear a simple explanation for the footprints. They could have been made anytime over the past four days, but she was sure any discrepancy in Dan's remarks had a similar innocent explanation that would come out eventually.

They strolled along for three blocks until the main street petered out into an unpaved path that wound down to a park by the river. The park was busier than the main street. Youngsters were playing on the sandy beach, boats were tied up at the public wharf, some brave souls had gone swimming and a lifeguard sat on a little wooden tower, surveying it all.

Farther back from the beach was a playground, which the children had abandoned for the seasonal pleasure of making sand castles on the beach. Susan felt a flood of memories at the old, familiar sight of seesaws, slides and swings. "I haven't seen a place like this since I left home!" she exclaimed, smiling, and hurried forward to try one of the swings.

She barely fit into the seat and got out before she broke it. "I guess I've filled out a little since I last tried one of these."

"And very nicely, too."

She flipped her braid over one shoulder and pretended not to notice how closely he was examining her.

"That seesaw should take your weight," Dan suggested, and they wandered over to it. "There's an art to this," he told her, and lifted the low end, steadying it while she climbed on. Then he took up the other end, and they began gently riding up and down.

It gave Susan a good view of Dan and put just the right amount of space between them. She looked along the length of board and found it hard to believe that the carefree-looking man at the other end could have a sinister bone in his body. He was completely at home in the rural, rustic place that was backed by soaring pines and outcroppings of stone. His rugged, weathered face seemed at one with nature, and his strong, tanned fingers gripped the handles. She could see the ripple of firm muscles beneath his close-fitting jeans as he moved the board up and down carefully to give her a smooth ride.

Just as her feeling of confidence was growing, he gave a reckless smile and said, "You realize I have you at my mercy, Susan. I control the balance with my greater weight. If I hopped off suddenly, I could give you a bump your tailbone would never forget." As he spoke he held his end down on the ground, raising her high, and held her there, gazing up at her, laughing at her powerlessness.

Far from being afraid, she was exhilarated by the game. "Of course, a gentleman and a scholar wouldn't do anything so childish," she replied.

Dan reflected that the brilliant blue sky above and around her produced the strange effect of a lady hanging in space, like a laughing angel. He found it the perfect backdrop for Susan. There was an ethereal, otherworldly quality in her ivory complexion and indigo eyes that spoke to his deepest instincts. Why couldn't he have met this ravishing woman at some other time? If she was safe, why couldn't he know it now, since their meetings would be so few and brief? And if she was not the innocent girl she seemed... Dan let his end of the seesaw rise, and Susan floated to earth.

He parried with "A nasty trick, throwing honor in my face." Now, why was she giving him that peculiar, mistrusting look? What had she learned about him? He'd done a little investigating himself and discovered that Anna Milton's domestics lived next door to the marina. They might have seen the equipment being ferried to Windmill Island. Damn, they might even have caught a glimpse of Golosov! He'd better talk away her suspicions, fast.

Susan's next remark gave him an opening to begin his explanations. "Not working today, I see," she said.

"Like you, I'm playing hooky. R and R is part of my reason for being here. I really should crack the books this afternoon, though. I've had about a ton of books and material taken to the island. And of course my computers." He knew he wasn't imagining the flash of interest in her indigo eyes, and he hoped that explained the mysterious parcels to her satisfaction.

A lingering question in her eyes prodded him on to other spurious explanations. "The man I'm helping came down with me to go over the research." He hoped that, if anyone had seen Golosov, this would explain the man's presence. Now he had to let her think that Golosov had left. "He had to rush back last night." He saw, though, that Susan still wore that wary look.

Dan had definitely said he was alone last night when he'd come to Sans Souci, Susan pondered, yet someone had changed that oil filter while Dan was with her. Or was it something else that had caused the interruption in the power? She didn't know a thing about pumps or motors, but Anna had said the generator was troublesome.

And Anna's friend at M.I.T. said there was no Dan Ogilvy on faculty there. The letters on his shirt caught her eye. She mustn't take all his explanations at face value, she told herself. "Have you been at M.I.T. long?" she asked.

Dan gave her a wary look. Had they phoned M.I.T. to check up on him? That question sounded highly suspicious. They were going beyond a nuisance and fast becoming a menace. "I'm not actually on staff. I do guest lectures for the physics department." He studied her to see if she accepted that.

"You said you were a professor," she reminded him.

"I don't like to boast, modest guy that I am, but they thought enough of me after a two-year stint at Cambridge to make me a professor emeritus."

"Oh, you must be famous! They don't confer that honor on just anyone."

It was ridiculous for a grown man to feel so gratified at her response, he chided himself. "It doesn't cost them anything, and it's considered good for international relations, scholastically speaking," he explained in a deprecatory way. That should give him a few days' grace. It would take Susan and Anna a while to make inquiries in England. Maybe he should contact Cambridge himself, just in case. Fortunately Susan changed the subject.

"Lucky you, living in England for two years. Isn't it lovely! Anna and I just got back. She's researching her next book."

They talked about England for a while. Dan found her intelligent and knowledgeable. "With your education, aren't you wasting your time being a secretary?" he asked.

"I'm more than that. I do research for my aunt, too."

"Did you ever think of writing a book yourself?"

How had he guessed? "I am working on a novel," she admitted. "Since Anna took me under her wing, I've caught the bug."

Dan got off the seesaw and held it without bumping till Susan dismounted. He took her hand to assist her. "Tell me about it," he said, and they began walking away, still holding hands.

"Well, it's a mystery, of course. Like Anna, I love mysteries. It's contemporary but based on a murder and a love triangle that took place fifty years ago. I call it *Old Lover's Ghost*."

"From 'Love's Deity,'" he said. "'I long to talk with some old lover's ghost, Who died before the god of love was born.'"

"You like John Donne!" she exclaimed. Even Anna hadn't recognized the quotation. How could a lover of metaphysical poetry be a criminal? she scoffed at herself.

"I see you believe the rumor that all scientists are Philistines. Not so, Ms. Knight."

Dan inclined his head to hers, and she saw that his eyes sparkled with mischief just before they softened in admiration. When he continued, his voice was husky.

"I've even been known to take up pen myself on occasion. Somewhere in my house in Boston there's a box of puerile love poems written to a young lady with 'tresses like Stygian night and skin of alabaster porcelain.' I didn't know in those days that alabaster and porcelain were two separate materials."

"She sounds like a very *hard* lady," Susan quipped, laughing. "Marble and porcelain."

"She was! Forged steel would have been a better metaphor. I don't understand how alabaster marble got its romantic reputation, anyway." They stopped at a coffee stand. Dan brushed her cheek with one finger. "Rose petals are more like it." While the blood began humming in his veins, he continued to gaze at her. Watch it, he told himself. Could any woman really be this sweet and innocent, blushing at his touch?

"Coffee?" he offered. "Or would you rather go to a restaurant?"

"It's fine here. I take double cream, no sugar."

"I take double everything, and to hell with the calories. You only live once."

Susan noticed as he strolled to the kiosk that he didn't have to worry about calories. There wasn't an ounce of fat on his tall, lean body, in spite of double everything and his potato chips and candy bars. He walked with the easy stride of an athlete. She wouldn't have thought a scholar would be so well-toned, or a scientist so familiar with metaphysical poetry. A strange enigma, this man who called himself Dan Ogilvy, she mused.

She accepted the coffee, and they walked to the shelter of a secluded rocky area surrounded by trees to sit on the ground. Susan leaned against a rock that was cushioned with lichen. Dan chose a tree and held up his cup. "A loaf of bread, a cup of coffee and thou beside me in the wilderness. Ah, wilderness! Ah, Omar, forgive my liberties. It ruins your meter."

"From John Donne to Omar Khayyám. I'm impressed! You really are interested in poetry."

Dan shrugged disparagingly. "Not am—was. The world doesn't produce Renaissance men nowadays. We're all specialists. Mathematics is the most beautiful poetry of all, though, and the hardest mistress. She monopolizes a man's time. I was hooked once I plumbed the mystery of things like the binomial theorem and the harmonic synthesizer. The latter isn't a musical keyboard—don't let the name fool you. It's an instrument for solving finite equations."

"Mystery's the right word." Susan settled in, enjoying their chat. "What's a nice man like you doing fooling around with finite equations?" She noted that the language of mathematics came as easily to him as poetry had.

Dan gave her a teasing look and edged closer. "What's a nice girl like you doing fooling around with murder? I'd never guess to look at you that you dreamed of blunt instruments and other lethal weapons."

"Arsenic, actually."

"Dare I use the word trite?"

"Certainly not. Cyanide is trite. And the murder occurred fifty years ago, so it has to be an old poison."

Dan studied her closely over the rim of his cup. If this woman was an agent, he'd have to reform her, that's all. He couldn't let her get away from him. When he spoke again, his voice was gentle. "You should be raising orchids or painting rainbows, not murdering people in print."

"How romantic." She smiled. "I didn't realize there was a market for rainbows. Where would people hang them?"

"In their castles in the air. All of us romantics have a castle in the air."

She laughed at his dreamy mood. "It's the best place for them. The ones we visited in England were cold and drafty and mostly taken over by the National Trust."

"And inhabited by old lovers' ghosts. When I die, I mean to fly across the Atlantic and take up residence in one of those romantic old heaps."

"I didn't know men had such foolish thoughts." Susan realized she'd just made an important discovery that would help in her writing: she'd had trouble writing about men, but they weren't all that different from women, really.

"You haven't been meeting the right men. And my thoughts are not foolish, just romantic. Men have always been the great romantics. Who wrote the *Rubaiyat* anyway, and *Love's Deity*?"

"The same sex that waged all the wars," she retaliated.

"While the gentler sex writes of murder. May I read your book?"

"No."

He gave her a curious smile. "No one can accuse you of not knowing your own mind. That was a very uncompromising answer. Why not?"

"Can I read your poetry?"

"How strong's your stomach?"

"Cast iron, but my pride is fragile. Until Anna tells me whether my book's any good, I'm not showing it to anyone."

Dan took her fingers and held them tightly. "I was mistaken to accuse you of knowing your own mind. Has Anna taken you under her wing or under her thumb? One day you'll have to trust your own instincts, Susan. You can't let someone else tell you what's right or wrong for you."

She gazed into the glimmering depth of his dark eyes, which seemed to hold a secret message. Was it a warning? As she sat, pondering, Dan set aside his coffee. Then he reached out, put her cup on the ground and twisted toward her. He was going to kiss her! she realized. He lowered his head till it hovered just inches above hers. That tantalizing scent of pine— was it coming from the trees, or Dan's after-shave?

His arms closed around her, protecting her from the hard rock as he pressed her against it with his chest. She closed her eyes, wrapped her arms around him and concentrated on the assault of his lips. They brushed softly against hers at first, teasing, exploring, tasting, like a butterfly after nectar. Her lips quivered expectantly. When she didn't push him away, Dan crushed her against him and intensified the kiss.

A riot of sensations swarmed over her. Through her shirt she felt the overpowering intimacy of his heat and the pressure of his hard body bearing down on her, molding the soft fullness of her breasts against him. A flutter inside her swelled to a tumult and it sent the blood coursing along her veins, eddying and swirling through her brain, making rational observation impossible. She knew only that no other kiss had so inflamed her.

Dan's tongue touched her lips. She felt the engrossing moistness as he flicked it lightly, exciting her with its gentle roughness. Her first feeling of alarm made her close her mouth. As he continued coaxing, cajoling with his tongue, he enchanted her to compliance. She parted her lips slowly, trembling uncertainly, and he entered to explore the intimacy of her mouth with leisurely abandon. She clutched at his back, which spread around her like a warm shield, holding her against the tree. She felt as if her lungs would explode if she didn't breathe soon. Just when she felt she could take no more, Dan drew back and gazed at her with a look of wild surprise.

Wow! he was thinking. Some alabaster maiden! He'd only meant to give her a light kiss, but the woman had flared like tinder.

"Conduct unbecoming a gentleman and a scholar," he said in a husky voice. "This is hardly the place for..." An experienced woman would have made light of it, he mused. Susan just sat, staring at him, a look of confused wonder glowing in her indigo eyes. As he watched, a wash of pink rose from her collar to suffuse her cheeks. He knew a blush couldn't be summoned at will, and Susan blushed divinely.

"A thousand islands to choose from, and you and I ended up on the same one, at the same time. It looks like fate," he said.

"I'm glad we met on an island," she replied. The words came tumbling out before she could think. He wouldn't understand—he'd think she was some sort of fool, but an island seemed romantic to Susan, with its intimations of otherworldliness, of storm-tossed lovers and remoteness from everyday cares.

Dan raised her hand to his lips and placed a kiss on the palm. "If you didn't already exist, I'd ask God to create you, Susan Knight. New York or Boston or even London wouldn't have been as perfect as our island."

Susan just smiled, satisfied that he had understood.

"We must do this again sometime," Dan said. "Say, this evening—if we can outsit your aunt."

She shook herself back to reality. "Oh, speaking of my aunt! I'd better get back. She'll be waiting for me."

"My equations will be lonesome, too. There shouldn't be aunts and equations on our fantasy island."

He rose and pulled her to her feet. Just before they left their private oasis, he touched her forehead with his lips. "That's for being such a delightful surprise," he said, and smiled softly.

The intensity of his look warmed her. Susan didn't dare ask him what he meant. The moment was interrupted by two young boys, who stared at them, then went away, laughing.

As the magic faded, she was embarrassed for having succumbed to him, and in such a public place. What must he think of her?

"I want you to know I don't usually do this sort of thing," she said brusquely.

Dan suppressed a smile. That prim speech sounded outrageously prudish, but she meant it, he knew, and on her it sounded right. "Then you have a natural talent. You do it exceedingly well."

She allowed herself a small, uncertain smile. "Do I?"

"Aces, Miss Knight. And now I'll let you get home, before the Mistress of Mayhem comes after us with a cleaver."

While they returned to the car and Dan gave Susan her packages, she forgot that he was a character of suspicious origins. They chatted easily about the quaint air of this small town and the scarcity of entertainment for future outings.

"It looks like we have a choice of bingo or the playground," she said.

"Use your imagination. They have a bicycle shop. I'll teach you to pop a wheelie."

"Teach *me* to pop a wheelie? Would you give Nureyev ballet lessons? I'll have you know I was popping wheelies before I could walk," she bragged lightly.

"Does Guinness know about this? You should be in their book of records."

"Well, before I started school anyway."

"Did I ever tell you about the trouble I had making my cradle?"

"That's funny. I didn't have any trouble making mine," she riposted.

Their banter kept Susan's mind busy until Dan left. When she was alone in the boat, flying across the water to Windmill Island, it first occurred to Susan that she was becoming involved with a man she knew little about—except that he didn't always tell the truth. And he was a very good kisser, she thought with a complacent smile.

Though Dan had mentioned hurrying back to work, she noticed he hadn't driven to the dock. He'd headed out of town. Where was he going? Maybe if she got home in time she could have a snoop around his cottage. That might help lessen Anna's wrath. As far as Susan was concerned, Dan was no more dangerous than the boy next door, but he was sure a lot more interesting.

Chapter Four

Susan pushed open the screen door of Sans Souci, rehearsing her apology for being so late. Anna met her with an apology of her own before Susan could speak.

"Please don't ask how I like *Old Lover's Ghost*, Susan, for I haven't had time to open it."

"What happened?"

Anna swelled in importance and announced, "I've been bird-watching." A pair of binoculars still hung around her neck. Anna had only a minimal interest in feathered creatures, unless they were required for one of her convoluted plots.

"On Dan's cottage?"

"Precisely. And I've spotted a mighty suspicious old crow flapping his wings there. A man, elderly, ugly as sin, wearing a blue shirt and suspenders—and trousers, of course! I'm not a voyeur."

Susan's heart sank at the news. So Dan had been lying to her. That kiss that had felt so right meant nothing. She went into the living room and put the newspapers and film on a table to give herself a moment's privacy to compose her thoughts. She had wanted so much for Dan to be innocent, but an innocent man had no reason to fabricate a tissue of lies.

Anna followed her in. "What do you think of that, eh?"

"I have a few things to report, too. Dan was at Westburg." Susan swallowed a lump in her throat and told Anna about the phone call that had required so many coin deposits and about his story that he'd been carrying books and a computer to the cottage over the past four days. "He said a colleague had been visiting him for a few days, but he left."

"Why would he lie, unless he has something to hide?" Anna asked. "We already know he doesn't teach at M.I.T."

"I prodded him about that a little. He said he only guest lectures there. The title of professor refers to Cambridge—professor emeritus." She added, "He *does* seem to know a lot about mathematics."

"It won't take long to check with Cambridge, but I'm not quite finished telling you *my* morning's findings. Nora Quinn got back to me after her husband looked into Sun Inc. It's a company, all right, but of very doubtful origins. It's a subsidiary of a holding company of a subsidiary—you get the idea. A blind to cover its illegal activities. And the price they pay Nora for her little shack! You wouldn't believe it."

Anna went to the window and peered across the water through her binoculars. Seeing nothing of interest, she resumed her tirade. "And incidentally, I spoke to Jed about the oil filter. He didn't replace it. He went to the generator to take a look for me. Whoever did it knew what he was doing. But who did it? That's the question."

"The man at Dan's cottage," Susan said dully. "Who else?"

"Exactly. Where's that film, Susan? I'm going back to see if I can get a picture of the man. You mailed the glass to Mr. Scott?"

Susan nodded.

"Good, then we should hear from him in a few days."

Anna began inserting the film in the camera, chattering while she worked. Susan was glad for the distraction. It kept her mind from dwelling on Dan's perfidy. Why had he bothered to sweet-talk her?

"We must accomplish two things at this dinner party tonight," Anna said.

"You're still inviting him to dinner?"

"I wish I'd made it lunch. I can hardly wait to get at him." Her eyes sparkled with pleasure. "About tonight, first I must get Dan's picture, and second, we must force him to invite us to his cottage. There's no hope of breaking in, since the large bird never leaves the place. Let's call Dan's colleague the Heron for easier reference. That'll let us discuss the man, even in Dan's presence if necessary. We might as well make the most of this affair. Excellent stuff for a book, Susan. I always capitalize on anything of this sort that comes along. I suggest you do likewise."

Nell called them to lunch, and just as they were finishing their soup and sandwich, a boat pulled up to their wharf. The woman who got out was a stranger, but as she was wearing a business suit, she obviously wasn't just a casual boater. She asked to see Miss Milton. Susan assumed it was a local reporter wanting an interview and took advantage of the free time to explore the island. She noticed that Dan's motorboat was back at his wharf.

Since this wasn't the time to do any snooping at his cottage, she walked the other way along the beach. The day couldn't have been more beautiful. The morning puffs of cloud had burned away, leaving the sky a clear azure. It was warm in the sun, but the breeze off the water kept her from being too hot. Unspoiled nature spread all around her. The Garden of Eden must have been like this, she reflected. And to complete the metaphor, the island came with a resident viper.

The shore curved inward toward the western end, and as Susan followed the coast, she lost sight of Sans Souci. The dense growth of the eastern end petered out to grass and wildflowers. A few violets and trilliums still blossomed, but most of the early blooms had faded, to be replaced by the summer growth of daisies and dandelions, buttercups and a few blue harebells for a variety of color.

She left the coast and ran through the grass till she reached the other side, then walked up the far side of the island. From the northern coast the mainland in the distance would be Canada. She and Anna were going to take the *Stella Maris* over one afternoon for some sight-seeing and shopping. The island sloped upward to the outcropping of limestone on the eastern end. The disappointing windmill soared above it all—marring the view, in Susan's opinion. The cliff wasn't sheer rock but earth and bushes and trees, with some rock, left over from primordial glacial movements, jutting up here and there like a giant, cosmic rock garden.

Susan stopped to admire its austere, rugged beauty. With the sun behind her now, visibility was perfect. Even with all the variables in her favor, when she first saw the man clambering over the rocks she thought that he was a large animal—perhaps a deer. A head shone a dusty rust color in the sunlight. But Anna had told her there was no large animal life on the island.

Her curiosity piqued, Susan stopped for a closer look. It could be a dog, maybe a collie. Did Dan have a dog? Then the thing stood up on its hind feet, and she no longer had any doubt that what she was looking at was a man. A bulky, rather awkward man. He didn't move with the ease and grace of a younger person. She recalled her aunt's description: an elderly man, ugly as sin, wearing a blue shirt and suspenders. Anna's Heron! Except he'd changed his blue shirt for beige, which blended with the rocks. When he wasn't moving, he could have been mistaken for a small boulder.

What on earth was he doing up on the cliffside? Climbing must be an exertion for an older man. If he'd just wanted exercise, he could have walked along the beach as she herself had done.

The man had stopped now. He stood still, looking. Good lord, she thought, he was looking at *her*! He might even have a gun trained on her, for all she knew! She took to her heels and flew down the coast. When she reached the flatter part of the island, she took the shortcut to Sans Souci. Her heart was pounding like a jackhammer.

She ran into the living room, where Anna sat, pondering a piece of paper in her lap.

"I saw him!" Susan gasped. "I saw the Heron, clambering over the rocks."

A smile split Anna's face. "A pity you hadn't taken the camera. What was he doing?"

Susan told her, and Anna rose and said, "It looks pretty suspicious that an older man should put himself to the exertion of cliff climbing on a hot afternoon." She began pacing. "It would be an excellent spot for them to erect some sort of tower for transmitting and receiving messages."

She stopped pacing and gave Susan a "eureka" look. "What an ideal spot for espionage! Every nation uses the St. Lawrence Seaway, including Russia. Ships passing in the channel could send instructions or receive news and pass it along with no fear of the message being intercepted."

"He wouldn't have to build a tower. The windmill's already there. He was very close to the windmill."

Anna's face blanched. "This is serious, Susan! I think I should contact Mr. Scott at once. Or perhaps the FBI is what we want. Pity I have no contacts there." She picked up the paper in her lap and fanned herself.

"What's that paper?" Susan asked. "Did your guest leave it?"

Anna gave a start of surprise. "It's an offer for Sun Inc. to buy Sans Souci and my half of the island," she said with a meaningful lift of her brow. "Nora Quinn thinks she got a good offer for her half of the island. She'll be green with envy when she hears mine. I'm tempted to accept, but I shan't.''

"Was the woman from Sun Inc.?''

"No, she was a real estate agent. I weakened when I saw the offer, but I didn't sign anything. I told her I'll think it over. I must think what to do.'' Anna resumed her pacing.

Anna's pacing was a familiar sight to Susan. It was her aunt's method of figuring out plot complexities. With her head bent, one arm held tightly against her chest and the other cupping her chin, she muttered to herself as she walked back and forth.

Susan could make out the words *FBI, CIA, electronic spying* and *nefarious plot*. She found it hard to believe Anna wasn't discussing merely a mystery book with herself. But there was real danger, and the villain would soon be arriving at their door to dine with them! That morning he had kissed her under the trees. They had laughed together, he had quoted and misquoted love poems to her, and her heart had thrilled to him.

Again she had to wonder why Dan had bothered to enthrall her. Was it only a diversion, to make her forget the mystery surrounding him, or was his reason even more devious? She remembered he had wanted to take her for a drive that morning. If she'd gone with him, would she be here, safe, now?

Was she letting herself be swayed by Anna's imagination again? What did they actually know that incriminated Dan? He might be an M.I.T. guest lecturer whose name Anna's friend didn't recognize. There could be a number of reasons why he would help a

friend conceal himself on the island. That man's
climbing up rocks didn't mean he was there to install
a transmitter or receiver, for heaven's sake. Maybe
he'd just wanted to see the windmill. She knew men
were interested in things like that.

And then there was Sun Inc. Maybe there was oil on
the island or under the water. Perhaps Sun Inc. wanted
to establish an island resort and Dan worked for Sun
Inc. and had instructions to keep the deal quiet. The
evidence was all circumstantial, really, the fruit of
Anna's hyperactive imagination. Dan had suggested
Susan think for herself, and that's what she would do.
But she'd keep her eyes open and her heart closed till
she knew more.

Anna stopped pacing. "He'll never let us take his
picture tonight if he's really a spy. That will be a good
test. I'll snap a picture in secret from behind a curtain
or something to make sure I get one, but I'll invent an
excuse to take one with his knowledge. I'll say I have
only one picture left and want to develop the film."

"And if he doesn't balk?"

"Well, if this is all a mistake—and I grant you we
have no hard evidence yet—then at least it's an interesting diversion." With another of her meaningful
looks, she added, "And of course Dan is very handsome."

"Meanwhile," she continued, "I've decided to wait
till I get a picture of Dan to send to Scott before I tell
him Dan's a spy. Another day won't matter, and I
wouldn't want to make a fool of myself."

Memories of the Dr. Buell affair must still be painful, Susan thought. She took it up eagerly. "Sun Inc.
might be legitimate. The conglomerate corporations

are so complicated nowadays they're worse than By-
zantine families."

She was cheered to hear that her aunt wasn't completely convinced of Dan's guilt, either; she didn't
have to lay all the blame on her own susceptibility. But
as she prepared herself for the evening, she knew she
was more susceptible than she wished.

They'd abandoned the idea of plain steaks for dinner. Nell was making a chateaubriand. A bouquet of
rosebuds graced the linen tablecloth, French wine was
being served, and rose candles would light the table.
Anna was wearing a long gown, and Susan decided to
make it a formal occasion as well. A long skirt
wouldn't be too much, and it would be wildly romantic. She'd brought a white silk evening skirt with her.
With it she'd wear the blue halter, which matched her
eyes. She drew her hair back into a chignon, recalling
that one of Anna's flirts had told her she looked like a
Spanish hidalgo in that hairdo. She wasn't sure she
looked like a noblewoman, but she knew she looked
good.

Her dangling Mexican silver earrings lent the right
Hispanic touch. Holding her head proudly erect, she
looked cool and sure of herself, she knew.

She went to Anna's room at five to seven. Her aunt
had told her she'd spent part of the afternoon snooping around Dan's place, taking pictures of the cottage
and his boat. Concealed by trees, she snapped any
boater close enough to come into range, in case Dan
had cohorts patrolling the shore.

Anna shook her head sadly when she saw Susan.

"What's the matter?" Susan asked. "Am I over-
dressed?"

Anna wore a shimmering gold gown and her antique topaz necklace. It would be hard for someone to be more overdressed than Anna, Susan mused. Her makeup was in place, eyes harshly outlined in black, cheeks just a little too orange.

"No, my dear, not at all. I'm just comparing the inequities of nature. It doesn't seem fair that you can buy that cheap little halter top off a sale table and look like a million dollars. I paid hundreds for this gown in Paris, and I look a fright. Oh, well, Dan's too young for me, so it's no matter. I'm going downstairs so I can be hiding when he comes. I'll take a picture of him from the partly closed dining room door as he enters—be sure you don't block my shot. That will leave one exposure for me to use later. I'll ask him point blank if I can take a picture of the two of you together, and if he refuses, we'll assume he's on police files somewhere."

And if he didn't refuse, Susan thought, then she intended to take it as evidence of his innocence.

They went downstairs, and Anna installed herself behind the dining room door, instructing Susan where to stand when Dan came in. Though only the hall light was lit, Anna had an extremely sensitive camera and didn't need a flash.

"It's nearly seven," Susan warned her.

"I trust he won't be so savage as to arrive on time. He should be half an hour late in the city, a quarter of an hour in the country."

Susan knew it was ridiculous to think of etiquette at a time like this, but Anna was a stickler for the social niceties.

Chapter Five

Dan arrived fifteen minutes late. He'd been doing considerable research into Anna Milton's background and suspected that a white jacket and black tie might be the thing to wear. More important, he knew Susan Knight was exactly who she'd said she was. His spirits were light that evening. He had to make enough of an impression on Susan that she'd remember him in the autumn when he looked her up in New York. Knowing Anna's penchant for sweets, he carried a box of chocolates for her, and for her niece he'd brought flowers. When Susan opened the door, he stood silent a moment, just looking at her.

His uncertain, blushing girl had turned into a sophisticated woman. She looked even more beautiful than he remembered but less approachable. He wondered how he'd found the nerve to kiss her. The bouquet of flowers he carried seemed a tawdry offering for this aristocratic-looking lady.

The sight of Dan nearly made Susan forget to stand aside for Anna's camera. The white jacket lent his weathered face and dark hair an air of elegance. He looked completely different from the man who'd first appeared at that door last night. The glow of his eyes on this occasion evoked in Susan no fear but only a memory of that kiss in the park. This cosmopolitan, handsome man had stepped right out of her fantasies. And if she wasn't careful, he'd step right into her heart.

The bouquet was of tiny pink roses arranged with babies' breath and fern, like a bride's bouquet. "I thought of you when I saw these," he said, handing it to her.

What a lovely way to be thought of, she marveled. "Oh, they're beautiful! Thank you!" She buried her face in their fragrance and inhaled deeply.

Then she remembered to step aside for Anna's picture. When it was developed, Susan would keep it even if Dan turned out to be a spy. She would pin it on her bulletin board, along with the magazine pictures of movie stars, whom she used to clarify the image of her heroes.

"Come in," she said, and he followed her swirling skirts, noticing how small her waist was. The twisted chignon of black hair rested on her neck, like ebony on ivory. "My aunt will be with us in a moment. She's just having a word with the cook. Actually Nell's not a cook exactly. She comes in by the day to help, but she does cook very well." Why am I babbling? It was the knowledge that those darkly glowing eyes were watching her.

"This'll be a real treat for me. I've been existing on frozen dinner and hamburgers."

Dan waited till she was seated before he sat down. He watched, bewitched, as a shy smile grew in her eyes. All her glamour and coolness faded, leaving the impression of a girl dressed in a grown-up's clothing.

"Oh, I should put these in water!" she exclaimed, and jumped up.

Anna entered at that moment, and Susan went to get a vase. When she returned, she put the flowers on the table and tried not to keep staring at them while she prepared and served a predinner drink. Anna had already begun a conversation designed to elicit some information.

"I had a most surprising visitor today," she was saying, and told Dan about Sun Inc.'s offer to buy her half of the island. "Do you know anything about the company?" she asked nonchalantly.

"Would it be a subsidiary of the oil company Suneca?" Dan asked.

"Very likely," Anna answered, watching him closely. "We're probably sitting on a gusher," she added, and laughed. "I can't imagine why else they're offering so much."

"That's certainly a stroke of luck for you," Dan said. "I imagine you'll take it, since you so seldom use the cottage."

When Anna replied, her smile reminded him of a crocodile's. "Oh, no, I couldn't sell Sans Souci. It's my little Shangri-La. I don't come often, but I like to know it's here, an oasis from the daily strife." She added more practically, "And if it's sitting on oil, the offer will only go up."

"They wouldn't really need your half of the island," he pointed out. "Oil can be pumped directly from the water. But it would certainly detract from your peace and quiet. Maybe you should think about it before you refuse, Anna."

Anna smiled blandly. "The Seaway authorities might not permit drilling here. It could interfere with the large ships using the channel. I believe I saw a Russian freighter today. It gave me quite a turn, seeing it." She peered at him out of the corner of her eyes.

"Probably carrying grain," Dan said. "They buy quite a bit of grain from us and Canada."

"I don't know why they allow the ships to come right into our rivers. Why, they could drop off spies, for all we know. Not that there'd be much to see here, on these little islands."

Dan didn't reveal by so much as a blink that these digs troubled him. He made a joking reply about the Russians stealing the fish, and before long Nell announced dinner. They went in state into the dining room.

"Isn't this lovely!" she exclaimed, smiling at the table. "Do you know, I'd like to take a picture of it. Why don't I take you and Dan, Susan? There's only one exposure left on the film, and I want to develop it tomorrow."

Susan looked questioningly at Dan. Was she imagining that wary light in his eyes? If he was concerned, he made a very rapid recovery. "Susan?" he said, and went to stand next to her.

Anna went to the other side of the table and snapped the picture. Susan's heart swelled with relief. Dan hadn't objected, so he must have nothing to hide. He sat across from her, with Anna at the head of the table, taking charge of the conversation. Susan knew her aunt had been deeply disappointed that Dan had submitted to having his picture taken.

"I was hoping to hear more from you about your work, Dan," Anna said leadingly. "Susan tells me you taught at Cambridge." Susan knew her aunt had not yet received a reply on her query to Cambridge.

"I did, a few years ago, but more advanced work on artificial intelligence is being done in the States now."

"Do you think there's much danger of someone inventing a robot that can actually think?"

"Any computer can think only what man programs it to think."

"Is it robots you're working on?"

"I'm working on the development of parallel-processing computers of the NON-VON type using binary-tree architecture. But I promise not to bore you with that. It can hardly be discussed in language that's intelligible to the layman."

While Anna appeared to be still reeling under this, he changed the subject. "You have a treasure in your cook, Anna. This chateaubriand is marvelous. You might be interested to know the dish is named after a French romantic writer, the Vicomte de Chateaubriand."

He continued with some amusing tales about this Vicomte's travels to Niagara Falls, where he discovered Cayuga Indians taking dancing lessons from a French traveler. "He wrote an epic poem about the trip, but if it survived, I've never heard of it. I imagine that as a writer you're interested in poetry, Anna.''

Dan proved to be interested in everything. He was a good talker, and Anna had no trouble keeping pace with him. Susan, for the most part, was content to sit and listen and occasionally add a few comments of her own. She was glad to see that Anna liked Dan. If they became really good friends, Dan would probably explain the little mystery about the man sharing his cottage. It was bound to be something innocent.

"Are you working on a book at the moment, Anna?" Dan asked.

"I'm planning one. My books take several months to gestate. Which leaves Susan with time on her hands." She looked expectantly from niece to guest.

"Then perhaps you could lend me your secretary from time to time," he requested. Dan was enjoying the evening so much that he hoped to have a few afternoons with Susan before the women left the island. Sun Inc. would have to boost the buying price. Anna wasn't going for the already generous offer they'd made that day.

"I'm sure Susan would be happy to give you a hand. She could do some typing for you, if that was your meaning."

It wasn't secretarial work Dan had in mind, but the glint in Anna's eyes suggested that some excuse to see Susan might be necessary. He could hardly admit he had no earthly use for a typist. "That would be very helpful, but I wouldn't want to impose."

"I'd be happy to," Susan assured him.

"Always glad to help a friend," Anna added.

Susan knew it was settled now. This was their chance to get inside Dan's cottage for some serious snooping. Her aunt's satisfied smile conveyed to Susan that she'd be safe; he wouldn't do any harm when the blame would fall in his own lap. Susan knew Anna held fast to her hopes that she was entertaining a spy and that she'd keep digging till she got word back from Bill Scott.

Dan found it difficult to back down without causing suspicion. "Perhaps one day when the weather's bad and you have nothing better to do," he suggested to Susan. Her smile of agreement warmed him like sunshine in the Arctic. In the insubstantial, flickering candlelight, she wore the air of a fairy-tale princess. What was it about her that caused these evanescent images to pop into his mind? Was it that she was too good to be true? And with all her loveliness, she was so unspoiled. That was it—she seemed to be untouched by sordid reality.

The jet black of her hair framed her ivory face, which was coming to haunt his dreams. Tonight, with the candle flames dancing in them, her indigo eyes looked as black as obsidian and suggested impossible fantasies. His gaze lingered on the curve of her cheek and on her straight nose, which was just slightly tilted at the end to suggest a trace of impertinence.

Her dainty shoulders, untouched as yet by the summer's sun, were pale against the blue top. A hint of cleavage was all the top allowed, but the shape of her ripe breasts were outlined clearly. He wanted to touch them, to feel their satin warmth against his face.

"The forecast for tomorrow is cool and overcast," Anna said. "What time would be convenient for you, Dan?"

He looked at Susan. "I don't want to get you out of bed too early. Say, ten?"

"That'll be fine," Susan agreed.

When their eyes met, there was a recognition that the meeting would be more than business. For Susan the knowledge lent an edge of excitement to the meal.

When they'd finished dinner, Nell removed the plates and went for dessert. Strawberries were in season now, and she'd concocted a fresh strawberry shortcake artistically decorated with whipped cream. Later, the group took their coffee to the screened porch and enjoyed the view and the breeze while they drank. It was eight-thirty, and the shadows of twilight were gathering, tinting the trees with purple. More than once Susan wished she could have a few minutes alone with Dan. The phone jangled inside, and in a moment Nell came to call Anna.

When they were alone, Dan turned to Susan. "I haven't dined like that for a long time. Home cooking. Nell's a treasure."

"We don't always dine in such high style. In New York Anna has only a maid who's no whiz in the kitchen. We do most of the cooking ourselves."

A comfortable silence fell as they looked through the screen at the river. The setting sun spread a crimson net over its rippling surface, with blackness showing below when the water shifted. One long steamer glided by as silently as a shark.

"I want to repay Anna's hospitality one of these evenings," Dan said, "but in the meantime perhaps you and I could explore some of the islands."

"I'd like that."

Anna soon returned, her chest puffed in importance. "Bother!" she exclaimed. Susan wasn't fooled, though; her aunt was delighted. "That was the Ogdensburg newspaper. They've learned I'm here and want an interview. I don't know how they found out. There's no escaping the press."

All they'd had to do, Susan mused, was read Anna's announcement in the New York papers that she was summering at her island home. If that failed, they could have read the interview Anna had given the Potsdam papers the day before, but her aunt liked to feel she was hounded.

"When are they coming?" Dan asked.

His voice wasn't sharp, Susan noticed, but there was an edge of curiosity in it.

"Tomorrow afternoon, around three."

"What a nuisance for you. Do reporters bother you much?" Dan listened closely for her reply. Reporters were the last thing he wanted at this time.

"They'll be after me only for the first week. Once the local rags have had their interview, they'll settle down." She drew a sigh and said stoically, "It's the price one has to pay for being a public figure."

They all chatted for awhile, then Anna rose and said, "Dan, would you think me a horrid hostess if I left you now? I have a few letters to write."

He rose politely. "I think you're a very fine and very considerate hostess, Anna," he replied with a charming smile as he allowed his eyes to trail off in Susan's direction for a moment. "I hope you'll let me show you that I can be a good host, too. I'll take you ladies to the mainland for dinner."

"Don't put yourself to so much bother. Just invite us to share whatever you're having. Hamburgers or chili—that sort of things tastes marvelous after a day in the great outdoors."

"We'll see."

Dan gave the lady his most charming smile, then, knowing her love of ritual and romance, he decided he couldn't go wrong with a kiss on her hand. He lifted her ringed fingers and lightly brushed them with his lips.

"Oh, my!" she twittered. "How Parisienne of you, Dan!" A trail of delighted laughter followed her into the cottage. The door closed, and Dan and Susan were alone at last.

"Shall we walk down to the beach?" he suggested.

"I'd love it."

"Maybe you should change your shoes."

"I'll just take them off. The pebbles are smooth."

Dan hesitated. He'd have to find some other excuse for a moment's privacy. "Fine. I'd like to pick up another of Anna's books before we go. Is it all right if I just slip into the study and ask her for one?"

"Sure. Go ahead."

Dan left, and Susan removed her sandals. Before he went to the study, Dan peered into the dining room. Nell had cleared the table, but the lights were still on. The camera rested on the shelf between the china cabinets. He was probably being overscrupulous, but Dillinger had said no pictures. He quickly opened it, exposing the film, and closed it again. Anna wasn't in her study after all, so he grabbed a book and hurried out.

"I'll pick this up later," he said, setting the book aside and holding the porch door for Susan.

They went out into the still night air down to the beach. Chiffon clouds floated low in the sky, showing patches of starry heavens. The moon played hide and seek with the clouds, now shining, now coyly disappearing. Tall pines stirred lazily, casting their resinous scent on the air, and beyond the shore the black water moved with an ominous beauty.

"I can't get used to the quiet here," Susan said softly. "It's so quiet it's deafening." She turned toward the Quinns' cottage.

"Let's go this way. I haven't explored this end of the island," Dan said, and put his hand on her elbow to guide her over the uneven beach, away from his cottage. "Are you sure those stones aren't hurting you?"

"It's like walking on marbles, smooth as can be. I can even run," she boasted, and withdrew her hand.

The primitive beauty all around filled her with energy that had to be spent. She wanted to climb mountains and swim oceans but contented herself with lifting her skirt and running down the beach. The scented wind on her face, the lapping water and the moving shadows conspired to enchant her. She never wanted to stop but soon grew tired.

Dan was only a step behind. He reached for her hand, and they both laughed.

"Some way for a princess to behave," he exclaimed.

"A princess? I'm just a poor relation. Anna's the princess."

"You make me feel like Prince Charming," he said softly, and drew her into his arms. "How did I get lucky enough to find you?"

The huskiness in his voice surprised her. Desire gleamed in the depths of his eyes as he gazed at her. His hands felt warm on her cool arms. The moon peeked out from behind a wisp of cloud, bathing her and Dan in pale light.

Dan put his arms around her. He'd been wanting to kiss Susan from the moment he'd first seen her that evening. Her pale face, framed in the black of the night, beguiled him. He studied it with solemn intensity for a moment, then closed his eyes and crushed her against him. She felt fragile in his arms, as delicate as a flower. Her face against his was a rose petal, her lips ripe cherries, full and sweet.

Susan saw the glitter of his eyes, then his face blurred as it came closer. She was still breathless from running and her breasts rose and fell rapidly, but at the touch of his lips the air swelled in her lungs. Then she felt the rougher material of his jacket exciting her flesh. She held him tightly to assure her reeling senses that this magic was truly occurring.

The first tender touching of lips hardly lasted a second. A fever seized her, and she welcomed the bruising pressure of his lips. He held her close with one arm, molding her full breasts against the firmness of his chest. His other hand moved as lightly as a bird's wing on her shoulder, tickling her skin. His fingers ceased their motion, then tightened, searing her flesh, while her insides melted.

A hunger grew in her and she opened her lips eagerly. He enfolded her with both arms, one grazing down her naked back before settling low, where he pulled their hips together with a rustle of silken skirt. The solid warmth of his torso was a harbor in the storm that raged inside her. It was something real and safe to cling to.

His tongue flickered over her lips, and she let him devastate the last shred of her control. She felt at the mercy of this man, whom she hardly knew. Her mistrust only heightened the excitement. Did he really mean the wonderful things his lips were implying? She raised a hand as if to push him off, but instead she settled it on his cheek, reveling in the roughness of his whiskers.

She felt his hand move between the closeness of their bodies. She knew it sought the rising swell of her breast, just at the edge of her bodice. A quiver stirred deep within her as he brushed his fingers intimately under the material, gathering one breast in his hand, enclosing it, gently palming its fullness with engrossing gentleness. Then his fingers tightened possessively, and his tongue probed deeper, plumbing the depths of her being. The quiver increased in intensity to a pulsing, throbbing desire. Susan fondled his hair uncontrollably, stroking his neck and cheeks with abandoned fervor.

When he moved his head to lower it to her breast, she heard him gasp. "Susan, Susan," he said raggedly. He pressed his cheek against her breast, moving it gently, flesh clinging to flesh, before he turned his head. As the exciting roughness of his moist tongue stroked her flesh, she felt the nipple come alive, puckering to his magic touch.

Every atom of her body responded to him. She heard her own soft gasp of pleasure when he drew the nipple into his mouth and stroked it hungrily. The smooth edge of his teeth grazed the erect nipple, and shock waves roared through her. This man was too experienced a lover for her, she thought. If she wasn't careful, they'd be mating on the beach like animals. There was such a fierce physical attraction between them that she had to stop, now, or it would be too late.

"Dan!" Her voice trembled on the air, half objecting, half encouraging.

When he looked up, his eyes were staring wildly, as though he were surprised himself at what he had been doing. "Susan, you're irresistible," he said, dazed.

She just looked at him, unable to think of words to acknowledge his praise. She'd always thought of herself as rather plain. For a man like Dan Ogilvy to call her irresistible took her breath away. "You must be joking," she said doubtfully.

Dan studied her with a curiously gentle smile. "Love isn't something to joke about."

Love, is that what was happening to her? Dan put his arm around her waist, and they retraced their steps, back toward Sans Souci. Susan was beyond words, and Dan didn't seem to feel any words were necessary. His arm around her waist, pulling their hips comfortably together, seemed enough.

"I'll get my book," he said when they reached Anna's cottage.

Wordlessly they went into the screened-in porch. In the concealing darkness he gathered her into his arms for a last long, scorching kiss. "Ten o'clock tomorrow?'' he said, nuzzling her ear. His tongue flicked out and touched it.

"I'll see you then."

"I'll see you before then, in my dreams. Sleep tight, princess."

He blew her a kiss and left. Whew! Dan thought. He was getting in over his head here. If he didn't watch it, he'd be asking Dillinger to let Susan stay on the island. Not much chance of getting any work done with that temptation next door. And poor Zinovi, alone all evening.

Dan unlocked the door and stepped into the dark hallway. A sliver of light shone around the door of the study. He went toward it and knocked. "Are you still awake, Zin?"

Zinovi was watching TV. He especially seemed to enjoy the commercials. An advertisement from a Mexican restaurant was playing at the moment, and Zinovi turned down the volume but kept watching avidly. They probably didn't have tacos in Russia, Dan mused.

"Did you manage to work out the optimum positions for the panels?" he asked.

The Russian nodded and mumbled, *"Da."*

"They must be installed very soon. You won't be safe here for long. Miss Milton won't agree to sell the cottage, and to make it worse, there'll be reporters here tomorrow to interview her. You'll have to lie low again."

Zinovi frowned and grumbled a moment.

Dan could hardly blame him. He knew it was tough, being locked up, but Zin didn't really seem to appreciate the danger he was in. Russia wouldn't spare any effort to prevent one of their top scientists from defecting to the west. He shouldn't have gone clambering up the hill that afternoon. "Miss Knight will be dropping by tomorrow morning, but I'll keep her in the kitchen. She wants to help with some typing," he told Zinovi.

What could he give her to type? Dan wondered. He'd noticed they had a typewriter at their place, so all he'd have to do is hand her the work. There was that lecture he'd given in Prague last year on world famine. He was supposed to be a computer expert on artificial intelligence. Actually the article touched on computerized farming, but she wouldn't know the difference. It was a good thing he had his handwritten copy with him; he could hardly ask her to type something from a magazine. He'd add a bit of malarkey about computers to the speech and make it do.

"The news'll be on in five minutes," he said to Zinovi. "Let's hope you're not on."

At Sans Souci, Susan and Anna also planned to watch the news, or listen to it, as the TV was still not working properly. But first they had to discuss the visit.

"Dan didn't object to having his picture taken, so I guess he's all right," Susan said with a satisfied smile.

"Yes, what a letdown, but I haven't given up on him yet. I'll get the film developed tomorrow morning and mail it to Scott, just in case. Dan pretended to know nothing about Sun Inc. and didn't bat an eye when I mentioned the Seaway being used for spying purposes. I hope he isn't just some innocent runaway husband. That man climbing the rock—there has to be something going on. You take a good look around the cottage tomorrow, Susan, when you're there typing.''

"Maybe the man on the rocks was just a trespasser.''

"He was trespassing on Dan's cottage, then. That's where I saw the Heron. Turn on the news, will you?''

"We don't get any picture, just snow.''

"Pity. I wanted to hear if they've had any luck finding that Russian scientist who disappeared from the meeting in Washington. It's mentioned in all the newspapers. We missed out on it while we were in London. Gobolov, I think the name was. What do you think could have happened to him? The Russians are saying we kidnapped him. The newspapers say he wants to defect, and the State Department pretend they don't know anything about him.''

"How long has he been missing?''

"Four days now. You may be sure the State Department has him safely under wraps.''

Anna took up the newspaper and scanned it. "Golosov is the name—they all sound alike. It seems Golosov is an expert on solar energy. He's been working on it with our scientists. As it isn't anything that involves defense, we're cooperating. That's a pleasant change. Since Chernobyl they'd be interested in alternate sources of energy.'' She turned to the entertainment section. "Listen to this, Susan. Nathan Hanover's new book has been optioned for a TV movie.''

It soon occurred to Susan that if Anna felt like reading, she might read *Old Lover's Ghost*. "Did you have any time to look at my manuscript?'' she asked hopefully.

"Tomorrow, for sure. I want my mind to be clear of other problems when I tackle it."

"I'm going up to bed, Anna."

"It's not late."

"I'll read for a while."

But she didn't read. She went to bed and thought of Dan. *Love isn't something to fool about,* he'd said. She hadn't thought love came in a blinding flash, either, that it hit you like a bolt of lightning and left you weak. She really didn't know anything about love. The love scenes in her book, she realized, were grossly inadequate, but what words could be used to re-create the enchantment of falling in love? It was beyond words. Thrilling, rapturous, ecstatic—they didn't convey the half of it.

Chapter Six

The next morning Anna took her film over to Westburg right after breakfast and was still away when Susan went to Dan's cottage. Anna had announced it would be a cool and overcast day, but that had just been an excuse to expedite her plan of getting Susan inside the cottage. In fact, the sun was shining in a cloudless blue sky, and the air was balmy. Susan wore a tailored white blouse that had a businesslike air about it and a denim skirt so she wouldn't look over-dressed. She scooped her hair back in a clip to keep it out of her face while she worked.

Dan was prepared for her visit this time. He'd even arranged to invite her in for coffee, to allay any feeling that the cottage was off limits. He made sure there was only one used set of dishes in the sink. The study door was not only closed but locked.

When he answered the door to Susan, he was glad he'd made his arrangements carefully, because he knew his mind wouldn't be on concealing Golosov's presence. Susan, without makeup and an elaborate gown, was just as beautiful as she'd looked the night before. Her complexion in the morning sun was that same flawless rose-petal texture. Sunlight reflected off her jet hair, highlighting hints of blue and purple and green.

The glow in her eyes wasn't all due to youth and good health; there was admiration mixed with it, he thought. It showed in her tentative smile and softly spoken "Good morning. I hope I'm not too early."

"You're late." He smiled. "It's a minute after ten." And the sixty seconds he'd spent waiting for her had seemed like an hour.

"You see how spoiled I am, working for my aunt."

"Don't expect me to get you in line. I'm putty in the hands of a beautiful woman.... The coffee's still fresh. Will you join me for one before we get to work?"

"You've discovered my weakness."

"And you've discovered mine." Susan gave him a frowning look. "Beautiful women." He laughed lightly and headed for the kitchen.

Susan followed him. Anna had warned her to look sharp for signs of the Heron, and she dutifully glanced around. There was only one pair of shoes at the back door, Dan's. One denim jacket hung on a hook above. She spotted a cup, saucer and plate in the sink. One half-empty glass of orange juice sat on the counter.

While Dan poured the coffee, Susan checked for other clues. A newsmagazine and the copy of *Abra Cadaver* rested on the table. The aroma of coffee and bacon hung on the air, with some other, less pleasant scent that she didn't recognize. But any cottage smelled a little musty after being closed for the winter.

Dan handed her a mug of steaming coffee and got a carton of cream from the refrigerator. "I don't have much typing to be done," he said. "The equations I'm working on aren't finished yet, and in any case they need a special scientific typewriter. What I thought you might do, if you don't mind, is type a lecture I'm preparing for September."

"Whatever I can do to help."

"There's no rush with it. It'll probably take more than a morning. I'll work on my equations while you type, and this afternoon I thought we might make a tour of the islands, if you're not busy. Anna's weather forecast was wrong, thank goodness."

"That sounds good to me."

"Bring along your bathing suit. The water's swimmable here."

"It's pretty cold!"

"Once you've braved the ice, you're allowed to call it refreshing."

They talked about the islands. Dan had been reading tourist brochures and mentioned other things to do. There was a guided tour of the islands and a night spot at nearby Alexandria Bay that had an outdoor dance floor. Susan smiled dreamily as she pictured herself and Dan dancing under the stars. She was surprised to look down and see her cup was empty.

"Time to get to work," Dan said reluctantly. "I'll get my notes." He disappeared from the kitchen, and Susan took the cups to the sink. The cream carton was empty, and she opened the cabinet door under the sink to throw it in the garbage. The oddly unpleasant smell she'd noticed was stronger here. On the top of the garbage bag sat a cigar butt.

Dan entered the kitchen just as she stood, staring at it.

"What are you doing?" he asked curtly.

She turned, surprised at the sharp tone of his voice. "Just putting the dishes in the sink. I didn't know you smoked cigars, Dan."

"I—I sometimes do when I'm working. It helps me concentrate."

"Oh." Why did that disturb him so? she wondered. Smoking was unhealthy, not illegal.

One could usually smell the odor on a smoker, but she hadn't smelled it on Dan. Her suspicions began to stir again. She ran water over the coffee cups.

"Just leave that. I'll do it," Dan said, hurrying toward her.

As Susan picked up the half-full glass of orange juice to add to the sink, some of the juice sloshed out onto her blouse.

"I'd better wash this off," she said. "Where's the washroom?"

"You can do it here," he said, and began looking around for a towel."

"Orange juice stains. I'd better give it a good cleaning. Where's the washroom?" she repeated.

She had the impression Dan was clenching his jaw, but he directed her to the washroom. Cleaning the stain took a few minutes, so she had some time to think. This visit, which had begun so pleasantly, had suddenly turned strange. Dan had acted very odd about that cigar butt. And he'd tried to keep her out of this room, too. When she'd finished washing the stain from her blouse and blotting it with the towel, she gingerly opened the medicine-cabinet door.

The cabinet held the usual items: shaving cream, an after-shave lotion, headache pills, toothpaste—two toothbrushes. How many toothbrushes did one man need? But more condemning than that was a can of denture adhesive. Susan's heart began to thud heavily. She closed the cabinet door and peered into the mirror. Her face was white, and her eyes were staring. She couldn't go out looking like this! She pinched her cheeks, forced a wide smile and returned to the kitchen.

"There. That should do it," she said brightly. She knew she wasn't imagining the apprehensive look in his eyes. But her smile seemed to reassure him.

"I'm glad no permanent damage was done. That's a nice shirt."

"What, this old thing?" Had she really said that! she thought. What was it about Dan that made her spout these awful lines? Nervousness, she supposed.

Their eyes met, and they laughed together at the cliché. "On you it looks good. Very good," Dan said.

His expression softened to admiration, and she knew by the sultry droop of his eyelids he wanted to kiss her. Whatever sham he was perpetrating, he did feel a real attraction to her. And the feeling was all too mutual. "Let's get to work," she said, to break the tension.

Dan handed her a sheaf of papers. "You'll want to use your own typewriter. There's no reason the typing has to be done here."

Susan felt sure there were more secrets to be discovered in the cottage. "I'll probably have to ask you about some of the words. It looks pretty technical," she added, casting a quick look at the manuscript.

"Actually, it's very straightforward. And it's just the first rough draft, so if there's anything you're not sure of, you can leave a blank and I'll fill it in."

"It seems a waste to have to retype it."

"I don't have a typewriter here," he said.

That pretty well clinched it, and the glint of triumph in his eyes annoyed her. "Why didn't you say so?" she snapped.

Dan's smile was more mischievous than cunning. "If you can say, 'What, this old thing,' I can say, 'You're awfully pretty when you're mad.' You are, you know." His voice was taking on that huskiness. "If I ever see you mad in the moonlight, I'm a goner."

"You mean angry, not mad," she corrected him, but her voice held no conviction. She didn't need moonlight. Dan was getting under her skin in broad daylight in a ramshackle old cottage that reeked of stale cigar smoke.

He didn't make a move to touch her. In fact, he folded his arms and stood with his feet apart, but his gaze, lingering on the curve of her cheek and the fullness of her lips, caused a tingle down her spine. She felt as if he were caressing her.

After awhile Dan said, "What time can I pick you up this afternoon?"

"I'd better check with Anna. She might want me to do something."

The corners of his lips quirked in amusement. "You're no competition for a reporter. She's giving an interview to the Ogdensburg paper. Remind her we're all here for R and R. And maybe even a little TLC.''

"Call me," Susan said, and turned toward the door. Dan was unfolding his arms, and she had a strong feeling they'd soon be around her if she didn't escape. "Oh, you don't have a phone!"

The words were no sooner out of her mouth than a phone rang behind one of the closed doors down the hall.

"I followed Anna's example and got a cellular one." It rang again.

"You'd better answer it."

Then it stopped ringing. "It has a few glitches," Dan explained. "It's rung two or three times, just rings twice, then stops. I don't answer it unless it rings at least three times. I'm conserving energy."

But of course there was a more common reason why a phone stopped ringing. Usually it meant someone had lifted the receiver. She listened, but if a man was speaking behind that closed door, Dan's voice concealed it. Was she imagining that he had raised his voice a little?

"I'll give you a call around one," he said, and took her elbow to lead her to the door.

He watched her run back to the cottage as though the hounds of hell were after her. She was suspicious, dammit, but she couldn't know anything for sure. Zinovi and his cheap cigars. Then, remembering the phone call, he went inside and unlocked the office door to see who'd been calling.

Zinovi sat at a desk, chewing a cigar about half an inch long. "Who was on the phone?" Dan asked.

Zinovi said it was Dillinger. Dan called his contact and learned that there was no money available to raise the offer on Miss Milton's half of the island.

"So, what do you suggest we do?" Dan asked Dillinger.

"I'll speak to the parks department. Maybe they'll help us with the finances and take over after the experiment is finished. I'm not sure going there was a good idea."

"You didn't have a better suggestion," Dan reminded him. "If you recall, we had about fifteen minutes to get Golosov out of Washington."

"I'll arrange something. Meanwhile, you might as well take advantage of the situation and continue with Project ISE."

Dan hung up and spoke to Golosov. "I'm going to risk going up the cliff and staking out the positions this morning. That's my end of the island. The ladies might be curious, but they can hardly stop me. And we're wasting too much time. If they spot me, I'll say I'm looking for Indian artifacts. The Indians were probably here a few hundred years ago."

Zinovi pulled a sheaf of papers forward, and Dan prepared for the climb. He knew Anna had left the island that morning and Susan would be typing, so that was a good time for him to go up the cliff. He planned to be back for lunch. He'd have to think up a new capitalist treat for Zin. Maybe the man would like ravioli.

At Sans Souci Susan put paper in the typewriter and began typing Dan's speech. His penmanship was clear and neat, written in a strong hand. She liked his composition style as well. He had a vigorous way of expressing his ideas. She had to admire, too, what the speech revealed of his philosophy; it showed a genuine concern for underprivileged nations and went beyond a passiveness to suggest ways of alleviating hunger. How could a man like that be involved in something criminal?

Maybe whatever Dan was trying to hide wasn't criminal, but she was convinced he hid some secret in the Quinns' cottage. He hadn't wanted her looking around, not even in the garbage bag. Why were there two toothbrushes, and the denture powder? She wished Anna would come home; her aunt seemed to be taking an awfully long time.

Anna didn't arrive till nearly twelve, and she was fuming. "Look at this, Susan! The man's a wizard." She threw an envelope of photographs on the desk. "The commercial photographer in Westburg develops pictures while you wait. I decided to wait rather than have to go back."

Susan reached eagerly for the pictures and flipped through them. Anna took a lousy picture. The photographs were mostly of branches of trees and shadows, with a few dim shots of boats, their shapes impossible to make out because of the sun's glare off the water. The last two shots were blotted out completely. What should have been the pictures of Dan at the door and Dan and Susan standing by the table didn't even have an outline. There was just a shiny pinkish blue blur.

"I don't understand," Susan said.

"The photographer wasn't even going to bother giving me these. He says the end of the film was exposed. *I* certainly didn't expose it while I was getting the film out. Someone must have done it on purpose. The only thing I can't understand is when Dan got at my camera. It was right on the sideboard all through the meal, and later we went outside. He must have sneaked in here last night while we were asleep."

"No," Susan said reluctantly, a heaviness in her chest. "He came in before he left last night. He said he wanted to borrow another of your books."

"You should have come with him!"

"I thought you'd be in your office. He said he was going to talk to you."

Anna's eyes sparkled with her fury. "What a cunning sneak he is. I'm more determined than ever to find out just what Dan Ogilvy is doing here. How did it go this morning?"

Susan mentioned the cigar butt, the two toothbrushes, the denture powder and the phone that had given only two rings.

Anna paced the room, one arm hugging her chest, one hand cupping her chin. "Bank robbers?" she muttered. "Hit men for the mob? Dope dealers, perhaps..."

Susan handed her a few typed pages of the manuscript. "I don't think it's anything like that, Anna. Read this. He's a scientist, all right. What surprises me is how little reference there is to computers. Just one page. He claims that's his area of expertise, but this is all about energy and agriculture."

Anna snatched at it eagerly and scanned the pages. "A good writing style. You don't often see semicolons nowadays. Such a pity. I've always had a special fondness for them; they look so dignified on the page."

"The writing's good, but I'm more interested in the philosophy."

"Oh, my dear, philosophy is all a sham. There's nothing in it but the rambling of tired old men."

"His attitude to life is what I meant. This doesn't sound like a criminal but someone who really cares about people."

"Is it his *attitude* you're talking about? You *said* philosophy. If you ever plan to be a writer, you must learn precision, Susan. Yes, he has a good attitude toward life. I sense a streak of anti-Americanism in his work, though. Quite a few reminders that Americans could do more to feed the hungry nations."

"He just means we should help them out with our technology."

"I wonder where he's giving this speech," Anna mused.

"He said it was a lecture. I assumed it was to be a guest lecture at M.I.T."

"You're forgetting, Susan, they've never heard of him at M.I.T."

"He explained about that. And he has the M.I.T. shirt."

"*You* have a shirt that says Oxford. The tone of this isn't academic at all. He claims to teach computer courses. Any fool can see this isn't that sort of lecture. It's a speech, not a lecture."

"And a very good speech, too."

Anna narrowed her eyes. "It's conned you, at any rate. Very likely that's the reason he scribbled it up after I insisted you go and help him. And why are you working here?"

"Dan doesn't have a typewriter," Susan said defensively.

"And you don't have any common sense. You lost it last night in the moonlight. You looked like a lovestruck schoolgirl when you came in barefoot. I trust that's all the apparel you removed."

Susan tossed her head boldly. "That's all I removed last night. Of course, this afternoon when we go swimming I'll be taking off more."

"Swimming, you say?" Anna asked. She didn't show any disapproval but rather a quick interest.

"Yes, since you're giving that interview you don't need me."

"That'll leave the Heron alone at the cottage. A toothless old man...I wouldn't be afraid of him," Anna said.

"I'm going to have a heart-to-heart talk with Dan. Whatever's going on, I don't think Dan is doing anything wrong. Maybe we can even help him."

"He doesn't appear interested in our help. And if he isn't a criminal, why did he destroy my photographs? Be careful, Susan. Do your swimming at a public place—either our wharf or one of the parks at Westburg."

Susan acknowledged the advice with a look, but she didn't intend to heed it. Dan had urged her to follow her own instincts, and that's what she meant to do, preferably in a nice, private spot.

Nell served an omelet and fresh asparagus for lunch, and as soon as they'd eaten, Susan said, "I'm going upstairs to change for this afternoon."

"I must get myself rigged out for the press, too, and speak with Nell about serving something. A drink should be enough."

"He's not coming till three. Will you have time to start reading my book?"

"How I'm looking forward to it! You have no idea. But first I'll give Bill Scott a call to tell him the glass is on its way and to ask a few questions about Dan Ogilvy. With luck I might hear from Cambridge this afternoon. If they refute his fine tale about being a professor emeritus, we'll have to do some more digging. I'll scout around the Quinns's cottage outside before the reporter comes."

"I see," Susan said. She knew that meant her book would sit unread again, but her attention soon turned to her date.

Chapter Seven

Dan was supposed to call at one, but she'd forgotten to give him their number, and it wasn't listed. She'd get ready anyway; he'd probably just show up at the cottage. She planned to wear her bathing suit under her shorts and shirt but was undecided between the two she'd brought with her. In public she usually wore a maillot, but for the privacy of the cottage she'd bought a skimpy bikini so she could work on her tan. It consisted of a black wisp of bra and brief bottom.

She put it on and studied her figure in the mirror. With a daring hunch of her shoulders she made up her mind, she'd wear the attractive bikini. After all, people went topless at lots of the beaches in Europe.

She wore a pair of modest white shorts, a loose, floppy yellow shirt that nearly covered them and a pair of multicolored Italian sandals. She got a beach towel from Nell and went to the porch to wait for Dan.

Susan saw him through the screen, gracefully striding along the beach. He wore the jeans and sports shirt he'd had on that morning. Susan ran down the stairs to meet him.

"You're punctual!" she said approvingly.

He moved his gaze admiringly over her casual outfit. "I've had to hold myself back. To keep from being early I went and got the boat gassed up and even bought a bottle of wine. Not your weakness, I know, but coffee's hard to prepare on an island."

He took her straw basket, and they went hand in hand toward Dan's wharf. The motorboat parked there, a newer, powerful model with a starter button and steering wheel, wasn't as large as Anna's. Dan got in behind the wheel, and Susan sat beside him.

"I thought we'd drive up and down the river first, then cut across toward Canada. There are some striking limestone cliffs on that side," Dan said. "We could take a buzz past Rockport—the cliffs are impressive there. It's just a few miles away."

"Sounds great."

Dan started the engine, and the boat zoomed across the water. The sun was warm on their backs, but the breeze fanned their faces, and the view of islands flashing past was stunning. Sailboats skimmed along like leaves flying before the wind. Conversation was difficult over the wind and roar of the motor, but Dan pointed out a few of the islands by name. There were private islands with cottages, government parks and some bits of land so small that Susan thought they must be just dots on the map. Dan drove a few miles east, then back to the west. In the distance a huge bridge spanned the river.

"That's the Ivy Lea International Bridge from Canada to the States. I'll bring you back to see it at night," Dan shouted. "All lit up, it looks like an electric bridge."

"It's beautiful!"

But the bridge was a few miles away, and Dan swerved the boat around before they passed under it, heading to the Canadian side. "That's the place I was telling you about," he said, pointing to a tree-dotted scree of limestone. A large white building rested at the top, overlooking the river.

"That's a hotel up there," Dan explained. "They have a good restaurant, too."

"Why don't we stop for a drink?"

"Good idea."

But after a minute Dan discovered he had to do some backtracking. Entering Canada would require ID, and he couldn't very well change his name at this point.

"I just remembered," he said. "I don't have my wallet."

"I have mine. I'll buy you a beer."

"You need some identification to enter Canada."

"Not a passport, I hope. We left ours in New York, and Anna and I mean to do some shopping in Canada."

"A driver's license is good enough, but I don't have mine. We'll do it another time. If you're thirsty, let's go to an island and have our wine."

"All right."

Dan veered the boat around, cutting a wide swath in the green surface of the river. They returned to the

American side, passing a publicly owned island with docks and a few picnickers on the beach.

"Why don't we stop there?" Susan suggested.

"I've found a better place, more private."

She remembered her aunt's warning, but she wasn't frightened of Dan. He cut the motor and drifted into the shore of a long island. "I don't know who owns this, but there's nothing built on it," he explained. "We'll risk trespassing, okay?"

"Okay."

As there was no dock, Dan had to drag the boat through the shallow water till it was beached. Susan took off her sandals and jumped out to help him. The water felt like ice.

"Let's do some exploring before we swim," Susan said.

Dan gave her a knowing smile. "It *is* cold, isn't it?"

She shuddered. "Freezing."

He took her hand and they began walking, first along the water's edge, then a little farther inland. The island wasn't densely overgrown, but was like a forest, with tall trees soaring overhead and wild grass underfoot. The ground was slippery with fallen needles and scattered with cones. Sun filtered through the branches, tracing dancing shadows on the forest floor.

Ahead lay a growth of wild irises, backed with a wall of ferns. The air was still, and the occasional caw of crows or screech of seagulls only emphasized their isolation. The scent of resin was strong here, blending with the perfume of wildflowers to sweeten the air.

They stopped a moment to admire the flowers. "This is how I imagine the Garden of Eden," Susan said. To her ears her voice sounded strangely hushed, as if she'd spoken in a cathedral.

Dan stopped walking and gazed down at her sun-dappled face. "You're how I imagine Eve." The birds fell silent, and his words echoed softly. She wasn't a fairy princess after all, he reflected. She was flesh and blood and one hundred percent temptation. But last night she'd been a princess. She was eternal woman, in all her infinite variety.

Susan felt his fingers tighten on her fingers and knew what was coming next. The sense of isolation suddenly seemed overwhelming. She wanted to escape, not from Dan but from this private garden, where anything might happen. Was it Dan she wanted to escape from, or herself? Or was it the knowledge that if they stayed here, something irrevocable would happen?

"Me?" she asked, trying for a breezy air. "I don't even like apples."

Dan accepted her mood. "You don't like apples? That's downright un-American of you. Are you against motherhood and apple pie, too?"

"Apples are all right cooked," she allowed, and continued walking, but retraced their path back toward the coast.

"And motherhood?" Dan pulled her to a stop and waited for her answer. His eyes, bright with interest, told her this wasn't just a facetious question. He really wanted to know.

"That's for later. I want a career first."

"Lots of women manage both. It would be easier for a writer. You could work at home, at least."

Susan averted her head and resumed walking while she thought about it. Of course he wasn't asking her to marry him, but it was something she'd have to think about eventually. "Writing takes a lot of concentration," she said simply. The path narrowed, and she skipped ahead, running to the beach.

Dan gave himself a mental kick. Slow down, idiot! You're scaring the poor woman out of her wits. The sun felt much warmer now that they were out of the shelter of the trees.

"Let's take a little sun before we swim," Susan suggested, and began arranging her towel on the ground near the beach. When it was time to take off her shirt, she wished she'd worn her other bathing suit. This one was too revealing. She was glad Dan wasn't watching her undress.

She looked from the corner of her eye as he kicked off his moccasins and pulled off his shirt and jeans. Wide brown shoulders tapered down to a lean waist and flat stomach ridged with muscles. A patch of black hair curled enticingly on his chest. Her gaze slid lower to his long, powerful legs. He must jog, she thought.

Dan looked up suddenly and caught her examining him. "Will I do?" he asked. There was an invitation in his look.

"In a pinch." She laughed and reached out to pinch him. Anything to break the sultry mood that was creeping in. She'd thought Dan would pull away, but he just stood, watching as her fingers touched him. "What do you do, pump iron?"

"That's for jocks. I play racquetball."

"That's for Yuppies."

"Yup."

His eyes held hers unwaveringly until Susan became uncomfortable. When Dan reached for her hand, she pulled away, feeling awkward.

Sensing her mood, Dan said, "Let's swim. The water will feel colder after a sunbath." And I need some cooling down, he added silently. The sight of Susan in that skimpy bikini made him hotter than the sun.

"I'll try, but I'm not sure I'll get in. I usually swim in a heated pool."

"Softie!" Laughing, he grabbed her hand to pull her into the lapping waves.

She hung back, and Dan used it as an excuse to put his arm around her. A ripple of excitement ran through her as his hand grazed her sensitive torso. It clung a moment, then tightened. Their hips were touching as they splashed out into the water. Susan knew that if she'd been alone, she wouldn't have braved the arctic temperature. But with Dan urging her on, laughing at her shrieks of protest, she was suddenly in up to her shoulders. After a moment she became used to the coldness and found she could move her limbs after all.

They swam out into the river, and Dan soon drew ahead. His powerful arms cut smoothly into the water, and his dark head moved from side to side as he surfaced to breathe. The swim was refreshing, but the cold water didn't encourage Susan to linger, and she soon went to the shore. The sun dried her quickly, and as she lay bathing in its heat, a languor invaded her bones.

After awhile she began to worry that Dan had swum out too far. Anna had warned her about the current in the channel. She rose reluctantly and went to the shore just as Dan was returning. As he reached the shallower water, he stopped swimming and stood up. The water fell in a silver shower from his shoulders, sparkling in the sunlight. The sight of him walking toward her caused a burgeoning heat inside her.

"I was afraid you'd drowned," she said.

He flashed a reckless smile. "Haven't you heard? Only the good die young."

"Are you telling me you're one of the bad guys?"

"Would I tell you if I was?" he joked, and finally reached dry ground.

Susan found it wasn't the possibility of his being a bad guy that bothered her today. It was the tantalizing attraction of his body, gleaming in the sun. She wanted to touch it, feel it pressing against her. And the smoldering glow in Dan's eyes told her that he felt the same way.

It seemed inevitable that he should draw her into his arms and that she should go willingly. His body was icy cold. She trembled at the first touch of his wet chest against her breast. She hazily noted that the clinging coolness of his arms around her should have felt unpleasant, but the difference in temperature only made her more acutely aware of him. The patch of hair on his chest excited her with its masculine roughness, but it was their bodies touching that sent that shudder through her. A swelling burgeoned in her chest till she felt she might burst.

With his cool hands he measured her waist, spanning it with his fingers. Then he slid his hands lower, over the feminine flare of her hips. It was easy, too easy, for him to imagine that Susan was naked in his arms. He pulled her closer and moved to savor the warm satiny smoothness of her nakedness against his flesh. Their thighs brushed intimately, disturbing his sanity when her leg moved between his.

The thrust of her lush breasts pressing his chest caused a weakening wash of desire when she looped her arms around him. He could even feel the beat of her heart and crushed her closer to enjoy it. Susan lifted her head, and Dan gazed at her for a moment before accepting the offer of her lips. The first touch was an achingly poignant instant of ecstasy. He felt her lips tremble under his with the tension of the moment. Her hands fluttered gently over his back. A delirium began throbbing in his head. With his tongue he pressed her lips open and entered the secret moistness of her mouth.

He heard a gasp as soft as a sigh. She quivered against him, her arms tightening, and his sanity slipped away. The throbbing of his blood echoed hypnotically in his ears, obliterating all other sounds. Susan lifted one arm, her fingers splayed over his head, stroking, teasing, then clutched spasmodically at his neck. He knew she, too, was losing control. When he felt her fingernails digging into his shoulders, he knew he must either make love to her or stop kissing her.

Dan slowly lifted his head and felt himself drowning in the pellucid blue of her eyes, which looked at him, dazed. She smiled trustingly, and the ache in his loins escalated to a compelling need. "Let's lie down," he said. His voice was ragged, drugged with desire.

Susan slowly shook herself back to reality. The wave of passion ebbed when he stopped kissing her. She was almost surprised to see the water out there. She'd forgotten where they were. There were quite a few boats close enough to see them, and she pulled away in embarrassment.

"We're putting on quite a show," she said quietly. She let her eyelids droop, to hide the love she knew must be shining in them.

Dan gazed down at the arc of long black lashes, fluttering against her cheeks. He lowered his head, brushing his chin against her hair. Every fiber of his body drove him to make love to this woman—here, now. He felt instinctively that Susan wouldn't object. So what was stopping him? Why did he feel this overpowering need to protect her?

"We're scandalizing the sea gulls," he said, and took her hand to lead her to his blanket.

Susan had a feeling so strong it amounted almost to a certainty that if she lay down with Dan on that blanket, they'd make love. She stood uncertainly, her bottom lip between her teeth. Then she looked at him.

Dan saw the shadow of fear that darkened her eyes. Good lord, she's a virgin! he thought. Joy and disbelief mingled with dismay. He couldn't take advantage of her, not like this, when they'd be parting within twenty-four hours. It would be weeks before he could tell her everything. Weeks for her to wonder and suffer....

"Shall we have that wine now?" he asked, and walked her over to her towel.

She was surprised to hear the peculiar strained note in his voice. What had happened? A minute ago Dan had wanted her as badly as she wanted him. Now he was calmly walking away, prying the cork out of a bottle of wine. She didn't know how to behave in this new situation.

"To us," Dan said, handing her a glass.

Susan had planned to ask Dan what was going on, and his odd behavior reminded her of the other discrepancies between what he said and what he did. She accepted the glass and sat on her towel. Dan left a discreet distance between himself and Susan and sat on his blanket.

She leveled a direct stare at him and said, "Dan, what's going on?"

He didn't meet her eyes, and his look of surprise was a trifle overdone, she felt.

"Going on? What do you mean? I just didn't feel this was the right time or place—"

"I don't mean why did you suddenly freeze up, though that's something else that confuses me. I mean what's going on at your cottage?"

"Nothing. You were there yourself."

"You don't smoke cigars. You seem to have only one set of teeth—your own, which don't need denture powder."

"That powder and extra toothbrush were there when I moved in."

"And the cigar?"

"A boater stopped by last night after I left you. His rudder got caught in the weeds near my place. I asked him in for a beer."

"You said you smoked."

"He gave me one. I took it to be sociable. Why have you suddenly turned into Nancy Drew?"

"I'm Anna Milton's niece. Blood will tell, I guess. That lecture I'm typing—it doesn't sound like a lecture. More like a speech. And it doesn't have much to do with computers, either. I don't like secrets, Dan. Why don't you just tell me what's going on?''

Her direct, trusting stare unnerved him. Dan realized that his worst fears had come to pass. The Mistress of Mayhem had smelled out some secret and wasn't likely to stop till she found the answer. He decided to admit something was afoot, though, of course, the nature of it wasn't his secret to tell.

"It's nothing you'd dislike, Susan. I'm just...doing a little job for the government. You read my speech."

She pounced on his words. "Aha! It *is* a speech!"

"I see you've studied it closely. Did it sound like the work of a— What is it you think I am, anyway?''

She continued to study him and finally made up her mind. "I think you're a nice man. I want you to tell me I'm right. That's why I asked you."

A warm feeling of love and relief swept over him. "Thanks for the vote of confidence. I hope I'm nice." He wanted to ease her frown of concern. Maybe he wanted to bask in her admiration, too. "I can't tell you exactly what I'm doing, Susan, but I'm not a traitor or spy or anything so glamorously evil. I'm a scientist. I like motherhood and apple pie, remember? Trust me, Susan."

Susan found it fatally easy to trust Dan Ogilvy. She couldn't see any trace of evil in his clear brown eyes, and it wasn't outside the realm of possibility that a scientist might be involved in some secret government project. "Will I ever know what it is you're doing?"

"When the thing's declassified, you'll be the first to know. And that's a promise."

She nodded. "There *is* another man at the cottage with you, isn't there?"

This was going to be the tough part. Dan shook his head. "Nope. Did you actually see anyone, or was it just the cigar butt and denture powder?" If they'd actually gotten a look at Golosov, steps must be taken immediately. He tried to sound unconcerned, but anxiety gnawed at him and lent a discordant note to his voice.

Susan noticed his wary look. She didn't believe Dan was doing anything wrong, but since he was keeping a few secrets from her, she decided to pay him back. "How could I, if there's no one there to see?" she parried.

"I thought Miss Milton's niece might have an active imagination."

"And twenty-twenty vision."

"It's a big island. There might be trespassers."

"Yeah. How about some more wine?" He noticed that her voice had hardened perceptibly.

As afternoon drew on a wind came up, and the breeze from the water turned cool. Susan's bikini was dry enough for her to get dressed, but Dan just put on his shirt. They decided to go home and gathered up their belongings.

"Don't forget your jeans," Susan said. As she picked them up she felt the unmistakable square of a wallet in his back pocket. *I just remembered. I don't have my wallet.* That's what he'd said when she'd suggested they stop at Rockport for a drink.

The afternoon, which had begun so idyllically, had changed as suddenly as the weather. The goose bumps on her arms weren't just caused by the cool breeze. She could believe a scientist might be doing some secret work for the government, but that wouldn't make him

ineligible to enter a foreign country. For some reason
Dan couldn't show his identification at a border, and
that didn't seem so innocent.

She rolled the jeans up to let Dan think she hadn't
noticed the wallet. All she wanted at that moment was
to escape, escape from the island and Dan Ogilvy.

She forced a cheerful smile. "Let's go!" she said,
and waded out to the boat.

Dan took her straight home. Since she'd drunk
some wine, the sun beating on her head gave her a
headache now. She was in a bad mood by the time
Dan glided his boat in at her dock. She hopped out
immediately. "Thanks, Dan. I had a swell time."

"I can tell by the frost in your voice."

"I'm just cold. I'll be seeing you."

They waved, and the boat sped on down the coast
to the Quinns' cottage. Susan watched it glide away,
half wishing Dan could glide out of her life as easily.
She hoped Anna was still with the reporter, but it was
five o'clock, and he'd probably left ages ago. She
pondered how much of her conversation with Dan she
would reveal to Anna.

Chapter Eight

Anna was still dressed in the white slacks and flowered Hawaiian shirt she'd worn to impress the reporter. Getting to a hairdresser from the island was a nuisance, so she'd covered her hair in a green turban. Her face was fully made up and she wore large gold hoop earrings. Normally Anna would have expected compliments for her effort, but Susan saw immediately that her mind was on more important matters. Anna wore the pouter-pigeon look that meant she had news to relate.

"Susan, thank God you got home safe and sound! I was about to send the Coast Guard out after you."

A surge of adrenaline rushed through Susan's veins. After a year, she should have grown used to Anna's dramatics, but she always succumbed. "Why? What happened?"

"What hasn't!" Anna exclaimed, handing her niece a magazine. "Page thirty-four."

Susan assumed it was a bad review of the latest book, till she noticed the magazine was *Scientific American*. On page thirty-four was an article entitled 'Feast, or Famine?' The first sentence jumped out at her, and she found herself reading an exact copy of the speech she'd typed for Dan that morning.

"By Easton," Anna said, pointing a jeweled finger at the author's name. "From the Massachusetts Institute of Technology. This is where Dan cribbed that speech he had you type. And you were taken in by his high-flown philosophy. Naturally you imagined Dan was a wise philanthropist. Easton is an eminent scientist. I believe I met him once, at a publishers' party in New York. He wrote a book about farming in the third world."

Susan stared at the familiar words till her bewilderment began to sort itself out. Dan hadn't written that article; he'd stolen it from Easton. Her first reaction was disbelief, her second disappointment. Grief washed over her. There was no longer any possibility that Dan's reputation could be redeemed. Even the glimmer of hope that Dan was Easton was stolen away from her. "You actually met Easton?" Susan asked.

"As I recall, he was a bald old fellow who looked as though hunger was the least of his own problems. A potbelly, he had."

"Then who's Dan Ogilvy?" Susan asked.

"An imposter, that's who. Didn't I tell you so?" Anna crowed gleefully.

"How did you find out?"

"Jim Zimmerman, the reporter from Ogdensburg, happened to glance at what you were typing. He recognized the title at once, since he'd read it just last week in the *Scientific American*. He looked through the article; it's identical. I told him you were using the article for typing practice—I had to tell him something. We don't want a reporter snooping around. I ran over to Westburg the minute he left and picked this up." She pointed to the magazine.

"Why would Dan go to all the trouble of copying out this article by hand and giving it to me to type?"

"To lull our suspicions and keep you busy so you wouldn't have time to do any investigating."

And he'd kissed her to lull her suspicions too. That's all it had meant to him. Anger began to grow, crowding out the bitter disappointment. "Of course."

"Hah, the more fool he, if he thinks we're conned so easily! Naturally I phoned Scott as soon as I verified that Zimmerman was right about this article. I always verify my facts."

"What did Scott say?"

"He was thrilled and complimented me to death on my acuity. The fingerprints on the glass will be run as soon as he gets it. He'll be in touch and let me know what he discovers. Bill believes we're dealing with an extremely dangerous man, Susan. No more dashing off with Dan Ogilvy. You're lucky you got back alive. Bill says we really should leave the island. He made a great issue of our keeping out of Ogilvy's way. I assured him we'd take every precaution."

"If he's that dangerous, maybe you should call the police, Anna."

"The local police are useless," Anna said, her cheeks turning pink at the memory of her dealings with them.

"The FBI, then," Susan urged.

"Officialdom must be notified eventually. I'll leave it up to Bill to determine exactly what we're dealing with."

"We won't see Dan if he comes again," Susan said firmly. She felt shriveled, as if the life had been wrung out of her. This was why Dan had been afraid to try to enter Canada; he'd known his name would be recognized and he'd be taken into custody for whatever crime it was he'd committed. How could she have been such a fool? She'd fallen in love with the bald, paunchy Easton, not Dan. It was that stranger's article that had given Dan an aura of benevolence.

"Not see him?" Anna exclaimed. "Of course we'll see him. I plan to exert every effort to help Bill."

Susan foresaw a round of foolish antics. She had no relish for anything that involved Dan. "He told you to butt out, Anna."

"The words 'butt out' were not used, I assure you. Our chat was very friendly. It was just my safety he was concerned about. Naturally we'll be very careful. We'll take no chances, but by hook or by crook, Susan, I mean to learn what Dan and the Heron are doing."

Susan knew it was important to learn this. Her anger solidified, and she decided she'd do everything in her power to bring Dan Ogilvy to justice. "Scott should send one of his operatives down to investigate," she replied.

"Send a man? He's coming himself. Didn't I tell you? Unfortunately he's winding up a forgery case today and can't come till tomorrow. That leaves us tonight to solve this matter. Wouldn't I love to hand Dan Ogilvy over to Bill in chains? Mistress of Mayhem Captures Dangerous Criminal Gang Singlehanded, the headlines would read."

"What, no help from me? I've found out a few things as well," Susan said, and told Anna about the wallet.

"That only confirms what I already discovered," Anna said dismissively. "I trust you didn't do as you threatened and ask him point-blank if he was a criminal."

"No, I didn't," Susan said, telling the literal truth while concealing that she had questioned Dan. How easily she'd been taken in. "Trust me," he'd said, and she was ready to abandon common sense and trust him, a man she hardly knew. "Did my speech sound like the work of a traitor or spy?" he'd asked her, or words to that effect. Of course Easton's speech sounded marvelous. Why shouldn't it? Easton was an eminent scientist working for the benefit of hungry nations.

Anna began pacing. "One thing puzzles me. I finally heard from Cambridge. They *do* have an emeritus professor called Dan Ogilvy. Strange, isn't it? Dan must be a scientist, all right. His description tallies exactly with their Ogilvy. Of course England is riddled with spies. Very likely that's where Dan was converted. I'm assuming he's a spy, not an ordinary thief or murderer."

"When did you settle on his crime?" Susan asked, her words tinged with anger. Dan was the cause of it, but Anna was with her and so received the first blast.

"We've discussed it before—that business of passing messages to ships in the Seaway. I hadn't spoken to Cambridge yet when I talked to Bill, but I gave him a hint of my suspicions. I tried to call him back but he was out rounding up the forgers. Naturally I couldn't reveal my news to just anyone. Bill will be returning my call."

Susan knew her aunt was in her element now. Nothing was dearer to Anna's heart than a mystery, and to have a real one to work with was a change for her. In this mood she wouldn't take much notice of her niece's unhappiness, Susan knew.

"We'll get over to the Quinns' cottage as soon as darkness falls," Anna continued. "There are any number of things to be done. I told Bill about the pictures that didn't turn out, but he said not to try to take any more. He agrees with me that Ogilvy exposed my film to light, the scoundrel. Oh, and there's the garbage! We'll see what they've thrown out. You can learn a lot from people's garbage. Well, the cigar butt, for instance! It's a whole new field, Garbology, I believe it's called."

Rooting through garbage held very little appeal for Susan, no matter what it was called, but she soon learned that would be her job, while Anna would listen at Dan's cottage window for clues.

"Scott told you to be careful," Susan reminded her. "Maybe we should ask Jed to accompany us. And we'll all wear dark clothes to avoid being seen."

"I'll get Jed to help. I wish I had a stethoscope to put to the window."

It was some small relief to Susan that Jed would be with them. She didn't think he could outfight Dan, but at least it would make it three against two. And the Heron, she assumed, was an older man.

They discussed other tricks to find out what Dan was up to, and half an hour later Nell came to the living room with the drink tray. "Jed's just stopped by to see if you'd like to buy some pike, Miss Milton," she said. "They're nice and fresh, and already cleaned. I could make them for dinner."

"Lovely, Nell. Would you tell Jed I'd like to speak to him before he leaves?"

Jed came in, looking out of place in his rough shirt and soiled trousers and smelling like a sushi restaurant. "Were you wanting something, Miss Milton?"

"Yes. Protection, Jed," she replied, and outlined her plan.

Jed nodded. "I've been wondering myself what those men were doing, scrabbling up the cliff."

"Have you seen them?" Anna asked eagerly.

"The younger lad was there all morning. I was fishing the north side of the island and spotted him. Measuring and digging it looked like. I drew alongside when he was coming down and asked him what he was doing. Said he was looking for Indian arrowheads. I never heard of anything like that on this island, but that's not your property, so I didn't say anything."

Susan remembered that Dan told her he was going to work on his equations. Had he ever told her the truth about anything?

"Measuring and digging, you say?" Anna asked.

"That's what it looked like."

Susan took this for confirmation that Dan was installing a transmitter and receiver for contacting passing ships.

"Jed, get into your boat and go back there," Anna said. "If the cliff's clear, would you mind climbing up and seeing what you can find? But make sure first that Ogilvy isn't around. He could be dangerous."

Susan knew that Jed didn't take Anna seriously when she was mystery hunting. He hadn't been involved in the arrest of the doctor whose daughter had diabetes, but five years before he'd spent a few days following perfectly innocent boats that Anna had thought were smuggling heroin from Canada into the States. It turned out to be some college kids who were living on the island and working at the resort at Rockport. Their dangerous parcels were their lunches and bathing suits.

"Maybe I should bring my rifle tonight," he suggested, to humor his employer.

"You do that, and I'll bring my pistol. In fact, I'd feel better if you took my pistol with you now. Would you get it please, Susan?"

Susan went reluctantly to fetch the dainty pearl-handled pistol. It seemed like a nightmare that Dan could be so dangerous that they had to arm themselves against him. It was Anna and her fertile imagination, magnifying everything again. But Mr. Scott, an experienced investigator who used to work for the CIA and who had contacts with the FBI, had called Dan dangerous. He hadn't traced the fingerprints yet though, so how could he know? Anna had managed to convince him. Just because Anna had decided Dan was a traitor didn't necessarily mean he was.

But he was definitely behaving suspiciously, and if he was doing a job for the government as he claimed, Bill Scott would have found out about it by now. Scott wouldn't be calling Dan dangerous. She drew a weary sigh and took the pistol downstairs. Anna explained to Jed how the safety catch worked. He put the little gun in his pocket and left.

"Do you really think this is necessary, Anna? What if something happens to Jed?" But in her heart it was Dan whom Susan was worried about. In spite of everything, she didn't want him to get hurt.

"Good old Jed," Anna smiled. "No need to worry about him. He was in the Second World War. Nothing much could faze him after that. He's a crack shot too. Ogilvy won't have a chance if he tries anything. But I hope Jed doesn't kill him. I should have told him not to shoot to kill."

"Kill?" Susan's cheeks blanched, and she stared wildly. She ran out after Jed and gave him the message.

Anna was waiting with narrowed eyes when Susan came back. "You seem mighty interested in Jed's safety all of a sudden, Susan. I thought you would've gotten over that schoolgirl crush on Dan Ogilvy. You didn't look so moonstruck when you came back today. He's no good, you know. Don't break your heart over someone like that. He'll soon be behind bars, where he belongs."

Susan found that while she had to endure her own censure of Dan, she couldn't endure Anna's. "You're

making a lot of assumptions here. You don't shoot a
man for plagiarizing an article.''

"Oh, Susan, what am I going to do with you? Such
an innocent. I hope your novel isn't riddled with this
sort of girlish nonsense.''

"You won't know till you read it. That'll be some
time next year, I imagine.''

"Sulks and pouts! My, my, we *are* in a temper. I'll
get at it first thing tomorrow—if Bill isn't here by then.
My own work is suffering too, you know. I'm supposed to be hatching my next book, but I haven't had
a minute to think about it.''

Susan accepted the olive branch. "I'm sorry, Anna.
I have a little headache from the sun. I'm going to lie
down before dinner.''

"Go ahead. You'll need your wits about you for
tonight.''

Susan knew she couldn't sleep with so much on her
mind, but she took a couple of headache tablets and
rested on her bed. She went over and over all Dan's lies
and deceitful behavior, trying to find a reason for
them, a reason that left him innocent. But there was
just too much duplicity. He hadn't told her the truth
about anything from the first night she'd met him. She
didn't even know his name. Maybe he wasn't even Dan
Ogilvy, the man that Cambridge said looked like him.
Maybe he'd stolen the identity, and that's why he
didn't want to pull out his wallet in front of her.

"Trust me," he'd said, but how could she go on
trusting when every way she looked, another piece of
deceit was waiting for her? Trust had to be a mutual
affair. Obviously Dan didn't trust her, or he'd have
told her the truth. She didn't trust him; she just loved

him. And she had an instinct that somewhere beneath his layers of lies, Dan really liked her. He was physically attracted, at least.

Or was that an act too? He'd cooled down very quickly on the island that afternoon. Was it possible there was one gentlemanly streak in him? He was willing to flirt with her to distract her from the truth, but he drew the line at seducing her. Or was the ignominious truth that he just didn't want to be intimate with her?

At five to seven, Susan rose and tidied her hair before dinner. She didn't bother changing since she'd only have to dress in the prescribed dark clothes for tonight's work. The aroma of cooking fish was not at all appetizing. Anna often boasted about the fresh fish to be had at Sans Souci, but in her present mood, the pike that Nell placed before her looked inedible.

Susan nibbled at it to avoid hurting Nell's feelings. Every bite felt like a stone as she swallowed it. They finished dinner at eight. The spying expedition was scheduled for nine, after the sun had gone down.

To kill time and to avoid painful memories, Susan decided to look over her manuscript. She noticed that Anna wasn't using this hour for the purpose. Was *Old Lover's Ghost* really as uninteresting as it seemed tonight? Or was it just that her mind was elsewhere? She read through a few chapters and set it aside, dissatisfied. She'd rewrite the opening, even if her aunt didn't suggest it. What she really wanted to think about was Dan and her aching heart. Originally all she had wanted from him was a friend for the summer. When had her expectations grown to include love? It seemed as if all she was going to get was a broken heart.

At a quarter to nine, Anna bustled in from the study and said, "Time to get ready, Susan. Remember, dark clothes. I'm going to rub charcoal on my face. There's some partially burned wood in the fireplace. It works very well."

"Is Jed here?"

"He's waiting in the kitchen. He tells me Dan has put some markers in the cliff, little red pegs set out in squares. You don't use pegs for archaeological digging."

"That's all he found when he investigated?"

Anna nodded. "Tomorrow he's going to fish on the north side of the island and keep an eye on the cliff with his binoculars."

Susan changed her clothes, and when she came back downstairs, Anna was already dressed in black slacks and sweater. Her hair was pushed up under an old navy tam, and her face was black.

"I'm melting with heat in this getup," Anna complained. "Wouldn't you know summer would decide to land in on us tonight?"

"At least Dan might have a window open. That'll make it easier to overhear them," Susan pointed out. Determined to do her duty, she forced her personal feelings aside for the duration.

Jed joined them, and Anna outlined their respective duties. She would listen at windows, Susan would tackle the garbage pail, and Jed would patrol with the pistol, ready to rush to their assistance if required. When all orders had been given, Anna told them to synchronize their watches. Susan shook her head ruefully, knowing there was no earthly reason for this. Anna just liked the drama of it.

More practically, Susan said, "We'd better turn out the lights in case Dan decides to call while we're gone." She extinguished the lamps, took her keys and locked the door.

Then the little troop went out into the shadows of night. Anna was so wrapped up in the thrill of the chase that it was left up to Susan to handle the details. She checked that Jed's boat and the *Stella Maris* were in the boathouse. If Dan strolled over, he'd think she and Anna had decided to go ashore.

Moving single file, they approached Dan's cottage via one of the back routes, Anna in the lead and Jed bringing up the rear. When they came out from the bush, they surveyed the cottage. All the blinds were drawn, but lights burning in three separate rooms suggested the presence of more than one person. Anna silently pointed out the route each of her troop was to take. Susan would pass the lit window toward the rear of the house on her way to the garbage pail and take a look in on her way past. She noticed that against the white cottage, their dark costumes stood out like a black cat in the snow. She should have thought of that. She hoped no one would be outside to see them.

She crept along till she stood outside the window. It was open, but the blind was drawn. It was a cheap old straw blind and some of the straws had sagged, leaving a space for her to peer through. Dan Ogilvy sat at a desk, punching a calculator and jotting something down on paper.

As Susan gazed in at him, her throat constricted with an aching sadness. He looked so...innocent, like a professor concentrating on his work. A lock of dark hair tumbled over his forehead. As he lifted a hand

and ran his fingers through the unruly mat of hair, she wanted to reach out and do the same. An awful loneliness welled up in her.

Of course she wasn't alone in the world. She had her family, she had Anna and friends, but she knew that without Dan Ogilvy there would be a gaping hole in her life, because she loved him. There, she admitted it. It wasn't just sex or experience or company on a lonely island she wanted from Dan. It was his love.

She shook herself back to attention and examined the room. The bookshelves and desk told her this was his office, and there wasn't a computer to be seen. What was there, as big as life, was a typewriter—and he'd told her he didn't have one! Nothing else in the room gave her any clues, and with a sigh of anger and regret she continued around to the garbage pail at the back of the cottage.

It was metal, and she had to be careful not to make noise as she lifted the lid and set it on the grass. By the light of the moon, she could make out a plastic bag containing coffee grounds, an egg carton, a bacon wrapper and a bag from a fast food place. The bag held four hamburger containers and two fries containers. One man didn't eat that much! Of course they already knew Dan wasn't there alone. Susan put the stuff back into the garbage tin and gingerly replaced the lid.

Her task had taken only a moment, and Susan joined Anna outside another lighted window. This blind didn't quite reach the bottom, and had likely been left up to let in the night breezes. It was an empty bedroom. The bed was unmade, but Susan noted that of more interest, the personal objects scattered around bore no resemblance to anything the elegant Dan Ogilvy would be caught dead in.

That dispirited flannelette dressing gown hanging off a chair looked a million years old, and on the floor beside it rested a pair of misshapen slippers. The wearer obviously had broad feet and a bunion on his right big toe. An old-fashioned three-piece blue serge suit hung on a hanger on the back of the closed door. Susan hadn't seen anything so poorly cut since her grandfather's funeral. She wondered if Nora Quinn had just left some old relatives' things scattered around the room. Then she remembered the Heron.

Yes, these clothes would fit him just about right. And the bunion would account for his awkward gait. She felt a little like a female Sherlock Holmes as she reviewed these brilliant deductions. Interesting as they were, however, they didn't tell her what Dan and the Heron were doing on the island.

As she and Anna watched, the suit swayed slightly, the door moved inward and the Heron himself came into the room. He was certainly no beauty, she mused. Tall, heavy, with a broad set of cheekbones that looked Slavic, he wore a white buttoned shirt, open at the neck, and gray trousers. He went to the bed, picked up a magazine and arranged the table lamp for reading.

Anna lifted her binoculars and looked through them, then passed them to Susan. She studied the magazine title and felt weak with excitement. The man was reading a Russian magazine. A spy! Her heart pounded so hard she was sure the man could hear it. Anna had often concocted a mystery out of trifles, but never before had her imaginings been so accurate. This justified the many times her aunt had been embarrassed at the hands of assorted officials. When the Heron settled in for a read, Susan and Anna moved along to the next window.

"There wasn't much in the garbage, but what do you make of that room?" Susan whispered.

"Shhh—we'll talk later."

The blind at this window was pulled down to the bottom and fit perfectly. "Playroom," Anna whispered. "The largest room in the cottage, and the likeliest place for them to leave those mysterious cartons that were supposed to hold books and computers."

"There was no computer in Dan's office," Susan murmured.

She knew they had to see into that room. The window was closed, but not so tightly that they couldn't get their fingers under the edge of the frame. After several tries, they managed to get the window open a few inches, then lifted the blind and peered into the room.

Susan couldn't make anything of the strange sight. Large, shiny rectangles of some dark material were stacked against the wall. The panels were about a yard long and two feet wide. She couldn't tell how many of them there were, but saw three piles, each of which held several panels. Cardboard boxes littered the floor. Beside them rested an even more suspicious-looking piece of equipment yet—some sort of motor, it looked like, and a reel of insulated electrical wire. Strange electronic devices that she thought might be meters were on a table by the motor. But oddest of all, there were picks and shovels.

The women exchanged a bewildered look. "Equipment for electronic spying, as I said," Anna declared.

"Those wires and things—could they be for a bomb?" Susan asked.

"Perhaps. I'm not just sure what those things that look like black windows are, but no doubt Bill will know."

Susan felt an urge to return to Dan's window. It was like probing an aching tooth, she reflected; she knew it would be agony, but she couldn't stop herself. "Do you want to have a look at Dan's office?" she whispered, to give herself another chance.

"I took a peek. Not much to see there. We've got all the evidence we need. We might as well leave."

Susan felt as if she were being plunged into a dark, cold lake. It was true, then. Dan really was a spy, a traitor to his country, and to her. He shouldn't have let her fall in love with him. He shouldn't have kissed her in the moonlight.

Jed suddenly appeared around the corner, slinking noiselessly like a hound. He beckoned them with one hand. Susan felt a thrill of excitement, though he hadn't said a word. Jed led them back to Dan's office and stood aside to let the ladies have first view at the window.

Susan pressed her nose against the sagging blind for optimum viewing and listening. The Heron had just ambled into Dan's office, carrying a bottle and two glasses. He spoke with a heavy accent that even an amateur sleuth could recognize as Eastern European. The word "comrade" was quite distinct.

Dan looked up and smiled. "I'll drink to that, Zin. Vodka, is it?" He took the glass and said, "To our collaboration. I'm glad we could agree to work together."

Anna jabbed Susan in the ribs and tossed her a triumphant look. Every word they uttered sent Susan deeper into pain, and Anna into seventh heaven. The man called Zin and Dan clicked glasses and both drank the toast in one gulp, in the Russian fashion.

Dan set down his glass and said, "I've been checking out the site. Digging there won't be easy. We're going to need a few men to help us."

Zin said something Susan couldn't decipher.

Dan's reply told her the question had been about them. "The ladies won't be around, Zin. I've arranged that—reluctantly, I must admit."

Susan felt another sharp jab in the ribs as Anna grabbed her elbow and pulled her away. When they were well beyond Dan's cottage, they felt it was safe to give vent to their anger.

"We won't be around—you heard that?" Anna exclaimed, eyes flashing. "Hah! We'll see who isn't around. *Comrade Ogilski* is the one who won't be around when Bill hears this."

When they were safely in Anna's living room with all doors and windows locked and the blinds drawn, Anna informed Jed, under oath of secrecy, of the Russian magazine. She told him to phone Nell and tell her he was staying overnight.

"She'll wonder why," Jed pointed out.

"I'll speak to her." Anna phoned Nell and told her they'd spotted an intruder on the island, and needed Jed for protection.

Anna then placed half a dozen calls in an effort to contact Bill Scott, even before she removed the soot from her face. Susan didn't know whether she was relieved or sorry that he wasn't at his office and his answering service couldn't, or wouldn't, help them locate him. Even the words "national crisis" and "red alert situation" didn't help her.

"We'll be lucky if we aren't found in our beds tomorrow with our throats slit," Anna complained.

"Why don't we call the police?" Susan asked. "We're certain now that Dan is a—spy." She choked on the last word.

"We're not sure just exactly what he's up to. Bill Scott will figure it all out, and we'll present the FBI with a *fait accompli*."

"Meanwhile you could go to a hotel for tonight," Jed suggested.

"I wouldn't dream of it," Anna declared firmly. "I'm not afraid of them. I'll lock my bedroom door and keep my pistol under my pillow. Sleep in my room tonight, Susan. There's no point in taking any chances."

"I'm going to take a shower," Susan said, and wandered out of the room.

The soot was hard to wash off. It lingered in the crevices of her nose and chin, but she found that scrubbing hard was a distraction from her lugubrious thoughts. She didn't want to sleep with Anna, so she decided to bunk out on the chaise longue in Anna's room. When Anna came up later, Susan pretended to be asleep, but long after the lights were out she lay on the uncomfortable bed, staring at the window.

She hoped Bill Scott would come very early in the morning and order them off the island. She didn't want to be there when they arrested Dan. She didn't want to see him with his hands manacled behind his back, like the offenders she'd seen on the TV news, trying to hide their faces with their jackets.

Hot tears oozed out of her eyes and slid down her face, but she cried silently, as Anna prided herself on being a light sleeper. All in all, it was about the worst night of Susan's life, and by morning she felt like a limp dishrag.

Chapter Nine

As if to mock Susan's mood, the sun shone gloriously bright the next morning. Toward the east the greenery looked gilt-edged, like a wedding invitation. Even the river flowed gold, its surface hardly ruffled. Dark plumes of pine tops swayed gently against the azure. The chirping of birds was so loud she could hear it through the closed window. It was a day for sunning and swimming, for boating and picnicking with a lover. Susan picked up her pillows and blanket and tiptoed to her own room to avoid waking Anna, who was still snoring.

A black mourning gown seemed the proper attire, but lacking this, Susan chose a flowered sundress and drew her hair to one side in a banana clip. It was time she pulled herself together and stopped mourning for a faithless man she'd known for only a few days. She must firm her resolve to do whatever must be done to trap the traitors next door.

She was hardened to resignation when she strode down to the breakfast table. She poured coffee, aware at the edge of her mind that the aroma of bacon and eggs was drifting in from the kitchen. They smelled good, but she knew it would be a trial for her to swallow them. The old aching constriction was still there in her throat.

When Nell came in, Susan forced a smile and said, "Good morning, Nell. A lovely day."

Nell placed the steaming plate before her. "It's going to be a roaster. Going up to eighty-five, according to the radio."

"Really? Maybe I'll swim.... This looks delicious."

It tasted delicious, too, but it went down like a plate of boulders. Never mind, she told herself. You need your energy. She ate what she could and took her coffee to the screened porch to wait till Anna came down. Her aunt had picked up a newsmagazine in Westburg yesterday, and Susan thumbed idly through it, though she barely glanced at the pages.

She'd flipped right past the picture of the Heron before it registered in her mind. The article was in the science section. A feverish excitement churned inside her as she read. Yes, their Heron, the man the magazine called Zinovi Golosov was a top Soviet scientist! Trying to quiet the whirling in her head, she scanned the article, struggling to make sense of it. Golosov had come to American to attend an international conference on means of helping the Third World.

Susan soon came across the name Dr. Philip Easton. She might have known her favorite philanthropist would be there. He and Golosov were leading a
discussion on solar energy. But how had Golosov gotten away from the conference and recruited Dan
Ogilvy to his cause? Or had Dan approached Golosov
and offered his services? The magazine was reporting
last week's news, of course. She and Anna had been
too busy in London to do much reading, and with
their TV showing only snow, they hadn't seen any
pictures, though the case had been reported on TV.

This was important enough to drag Anna out of
bed, she decided, and was just about to go inside when
she saw Dan striding along the beach toward Sans
Souci. Her instinctive surge of joy soon turned to
sadness, then hardened to anger. He wouldn't be
coming in the brightness of day to do any harm, she
knew. Jed and Nell were in the kitchen, so she could
risk talking to him for a minute. Maybe she'd learn
something.

He didn't look as if he planned to stop, anyway,
though he glanced toward the porch. When he saw her
silhouette against the screen, he turned toward the
cottage.

"Good morning," he called, waving.

The sun struck him full in the face, coloring him in
a golden glow. He wore a short-sleeved T-shirt and
looked vigorously healthy and dangerously attractive. He hurried forward, running the last little distance. She stifled the thrill of pleasure his appearance
still caused. Time to grow up! she told herself, sup-
pressing her emotions and hardening her heart against

him as she hastily stuffed the magazine under the sofa.
When he got to the door, he found it was still locked.

"Where you expecting the bogeyman?" he laughed.
"One of the benefits of living here is that you don't
have to lock your doors."

But she remembered *he'd* locked his back screen
door. She drew the bolt and he came in. "It's going to
be a scorcher," he said.

"Rather hot for a walk along the beach?" Her tone
made it a question. No doubt he had some important
reason for that walk. Checking for the approach of a
freighter, perhaps?

"I was hoping I'd see you...alone."

The insinuation in his voice caused a spasm of an-
ticipation just before the alarm bells rang in her head.
Fortunately she didn't have to reply. Nell had spotted
Dan and hurried in to see if Susan was safe. "Would
Mr. Ogilvy like some coffee?" she asked, to account
for her visit.

"That'd be nice. Thanks." Dan smiled.

Susan just looked at him. She couldn't think of
anything to say. "How could you?" were the words
that crowded her throat, but she couldn't say that.

"Mind if I grab a seat?" Dan asked, and sat down.
"I've been thinking how I can entertain you and
Anna," he continued in a normal, friendly voice. But
it wasn't the intimate voice he'd first used. Had he
sensed her withdrawal? He was looking at her oddly
now—she had to say something.

"I see the threat of my cooking's thrown you," Dan
went on. "Actually, I grill a pretty good steak. I'm
hoping you and Anna will join me for a barbecue tonight."

It was safe to accept, Susan knew. In fact, it would put Dan off his guard and let him believe they weren't aware of who he was. "Good. I'll tell Anna." Did her voice sound as strained to him as it did to her?

"Anna did tell me not to go to any extraordinary pains." He chatted on.

Nell brought the coffee. While Dan prepared it to his liking, Susan stole a long gaze at him. His dark hair, slightly ruffled from his walk, gave him a boyish look. Brown eyes always seemed friendly to Susan, but now she knew his friendliness was all an act. Well, she, too, could act. She would convince him she was a lovesick female and Anna was just a harmless writer. And while she was at it, she would make him squirm a little.

"I do hope you won't make us eat our steak outdoors," she said. "It's so unpleasant, with the bugs and mosquitoes and wind, you know." Let's see how you plan to keep us out of your house tonight, Comrade Ogilvy!

He didn't object, but she noticed the odd look that passed over his face.

Was that an innocent remark, Dan was wondering, or were the ladies curious to get into his cottage? He decided to sound her out. "The cottage'll be like an oven by dinnertime."

"Why don't we all have a swim first to cool down?"

They were curious, definitely. Not that it mattered. Unfortunately there wasn't going to be any barbecue, but talking about one would lull their suspicions, and it gave him an excuse to be with Susan one more time. This summer, which he'd been looking forward to, had become more agony than pleasure. And the rea-

son for it was sitting so close he could kiss her. If
only...

Dillinger hadn't managed to arrange a deal to buy
the rest of the island and was hatching a plan to re-
move the ladies forcibly. That was bound to leave a
bad taste in their mouths. Pulling the required strings,
he'd said, should be accomplished by this afternoon.
So this was probably the last time he'd see Susan for a
few months.

He shook himself back to the present and said,
"The water's still pretty cold."

"It wasn't too cold yesterday. We swam at the
island. Have you forgotten?" Susan said, gazing
deeply into his eyes. Had he forgotten kissing her? She
didn't think so, for a dreamy expression had come over
his face. She decided to goad him further. A pout was
the pose called for now. "I thought I might see you
last night."

"I wanted to see you."

"Why didn't you call?"

"I did! I phoned twice, and there was no answer."
His brows drew together in a pucker. What was going
on here? Teasing and pouts weren't Susan's usual way
of behaving. She almost acted as though...as though
she were acting. And now she looked a little embarrassed. "Were you here all the time?"

"We went over to Westburg for the late movie. Our
TV doesn't work. We were here till nearly nine," she
replied quickly.

"You're a Clint Eastwood fan, are you?"

"Isn't everybody?" she said lightly.

Very interesting! Dan mused. Eastwood wasn't playing at Westburg. Where had she really been? "I didn't think he'd be Anna's type."

"I twisted her arm a little."

"If you'd care to give mine a twist, I might be talked into making your day."

She looked surprised. "What did you have in mind?"

"Relieving you from typing those lecture notes I gave you. I'm feeling a little guilty about that. I'll mail them to my secretary." He'd been horrified to see the current issue of *Scientific American* sitting on the newsstand in Westburg. He'd bought the two remaining copies, but the owner had told him there had been four. It wasn't popular reading for the layman, but he knew a mystery writer might decide to give it a try. Something had certainly happened, for Susan wasn't acting like herself today, and why would she lie about going to the movie last night?

"I'm nearly finished typing it," she said, not meeting his eyes. He was the one in the wrong, but she wasn't used to lying and she felt guilty. Guilty and betrayed and deeply saddened. She drew a deep sigh. Life had become so complicated!

That sigh caused Dan a pang of futile regret. "Susan." His voice was a gentle croon. He set his coffee aside and sat beside her on the rattan settee. He tried to take her hand, but she pulled it away. "What's the matter? Did you get up on the wrong side of the bed?" he asked coaxingly, moving closer to her. Susan withdrew to the far end of the settee.

Dan moved along till he had her cornered, then he put an arm around her shoulder. At this close range he could hardly control his urge to kiss her. "Why don't we go for a little walk before it gets too hot?"

The husky burr was back in his voice, she realized, and it sent shivers of anticipation up her spine. The temptation was still there. Even knowing what she knew about him, she felt a strong urge to accept. She could tell what he had in mind: *Let's go where we can be alone for a little while.* The heat of his body tempted her to accept. He inclined his head till their foreheads touched and settled his hand on the nape of her neck, fondling her hair. She knew she should move away from him, but before she could he unfastened her hair clip and drew his fingers through her loosely flowing locks.

Dan reflected that her hair felt like silk threads as he wound it around his fingers. "I feel poetic urgings when I touch this," he said.

"You won't even have to exercise your brain. You've already done an ode to black hair. 'Stygian night' will do equally well for mine."

"I've outgrown my classical period."

She felt heated as his thumb grazed her cheek engrossingly. His voice was as soft as a breeze.

"I'm through with alabaster maidens. What goes with rose petals?"

A weakening wave of longing washed over her. She had to force herself to withstand his temptation. "A garbage pail," she said snidely. "Once the petals start falling, that's where roses end up." The roses he'd given her had been a fitting gift—so temporary. They were already turning brown around the edges.

Dan quirked an eyebrow at her. "Talk about rain-ing on a guy's parade! I hope you're not always this grumpy in the morning."

This oblique suggestion that they might be sharing mornings—how it would have thrilled her a few days ago, she thought sadly. Now it only hardened her an-ger. "I don't foresee any problems there."

"You're right. I've already told you how beautiful you are when you're mad. I'll just look and not lis-ten."

Susan picked up a newspaper and began fanning herself as though she hadn't heard him. "It's hot."

"If you'd like to slip into that sexy black bikini you wore yesterday..." In less than a day Susan would be gone, and he wanted to hold her in his arms once more before she left.

She jumped up from the settee and glared at him. There were dozens of accusations she wanted to hurl at him, but she couldn't admit she knew so much about him. In frustration she heard herself say, "For your information, that black bathing suit is not sexy."

Dan looked at her, surprised. "I beg to differ. It probably lacks a certain something when it's sitting in the drawer. When you're wearing it, it's sexy. Very sexy." He rose and pulled Susan back down beside him. "Something's the matter between us, and I have a pretty good idea what it is. Yesterday you asked me what I was doing here. I'm sure you remember what I told you. It's a job for the government."

She raised her eyes and gave him a look of deep distrust. "Whose government?" The words popped out before she could stop them.

She saw the flash of angry surprise in his eyes. His nostrils quivered, and his body stiffened. "What are you talking about?" The question lashed out like a whip.

Suddenly she found it easy to believe all her suspicions. Dan *was* dangerous. She swallowed nervously.

Indignation buzzed in his voice as he asked, "Is that what you think of me?"

Just then Anna came floating into the porch. "Dan, how kind of you to drop in on us. Have you had breakfast?"

He made a determined effort to hide his anger as he replied, "Nell offered me coffee." His cup was still full, but he didn't sit down again. "I'm afraid I'm just leaving, Anna, but I hope to see you this evening. Susan will tell you about it."

"Must you go?" Anna asked.

The door was already open. "I'm afraid I must." He gave Susan one last hard look, then turned to her aunt. "*You'll* miss me when I'm gone, won't you, Anna?" He pulled open the door and strode out.

"Well!" Anna exclaimed when they were alone. "What got into him? I hope you haven't given anything away, Susan. Dan looked ready to chew nails."

To avoid a long cross-examination, Susan said, "Actually, we were arguing about my bikini."

"Oh, dear, when men start complaining about a woman revealing her charms, it means they're feeling possessive."

Apparently Dan hadn't been feeling possessive, then, Susan thought. Far from it. She retrieved the newsmagazine from under the settee and handed it to Anna. "We have a name for the Heron now," she said. "Zinovi Golosov, an important Russian scientist. Golosov slipped away from the conference and is setting up an electronic spy network right here, on Windmill Island."

Anna glanced at the picture. "What a blessing I decided to come here this summer, or no one would ever have been any the wiser."

"Dan tried to get Easton's speech back from me. He must have seen it in *Scientific American*. Oh, incidentally, he invited us to dinner tonight." She added the pertinent details.

"A barbecue, huh? And he dug in his heels about letting us into the house. Highly suspicious."

"If you happen to see Dan today, we were at a Clint Eastwood movie last night when he phoned."

"Clint Eastwood isn't playing in Westburg!" Anna exclaimed.

"No!" Susan gasped. He had acted so enamored, but he'd only come to test her!

"He was *testing* you, Susan. He must suspect we're on to him."

"We better call the police," Susan said. Anna seemed to consider it a moment this time. "Don't try to be one of your own heroines, Anna. This is too dangerous."

"But what a crowning glory for my career! Think of the publicity. And what a chance for Bill to make a name for himself, too. I'll phone Bill and tell him to get moving." She went into her office to make the call, and Susan followed, listening at her elbow.

"Bill, Anna here. I have some interesting news on the Heron."

Bill Scott was deeply involved in his forgery case and was in no mood to coddle Miss Milton. "I'm a busy man, Annie. Cut to the chase," Susan heard him say curtly.

Anna's breast swelled in indignation. "Too busy to hear where Zinovi Golosov is hiding? Then perhaps you'd be kind enough to give me the phone number of the head of the FBI."

"Golosov! You're putting me on."

"Never mind. I'll have the operator get me the number."

"Wait! You're sure the guy's Golosov? My rear end'll be up for grabs if you're leading me astray here."

"I've seen him with my own eyes," she assured him, and added enough details that Scott believed her.

"So that's where Golosov's gotten to! He vanished from his hotel without a trace the day the conference wound up. The FBI's managed to keep a lid on his disappearance. Even the press haven't been able to find him."

"Perhaps we should notify the FBI?" she suggested.

"That bunch of Keystone Cops? I suggest you and I handle it. There's ink in this for both of us. We'll be on page one in every newspaper in the country if we can break this. I'll hop right over to your place. You'd better give me L. and L. on that island, Anna." Anna and Susan exchanged a perplexed frown. "Latitude and longitude," he added. "I'll hop a helicopter to the closest landing strip and drive or take a boat—or swim, if necessary."

"Westburg, New York," Anna told him. "I'll be waiting at the marina with my boat. How long will it take you?"

"I just left. No, on second thought, you stay put till I get back to you. I'll put out a few feelers first and see if the FBI knows anything about this. I don't want to find myself in the crossfire if they're running a C.O."

"You think there's a covert operation going down?" she asked sagely.

"It could be. I'll get back to you. Don't leave the phone. *Capisce*?"

"Roger!"

"Over and out. I won't forget you for this, Annie baby."

While Anna stared at the humming receiver, Susan said worriedly, "He sounds kind of breezy."

"Bill knows what he's doing. I wish I knew someone at the FBI, though. I don't want to get in their bad books, but on the other hand I don't like to call and be put on hold by some condescending secretary. Well, at least I can make sure the boat's ready to go and fetch Bill. You'll keep close to the phone, Susan?"

The phone rang not ten minutes later. "I've got to talk to Annie," Bill Scott said. He sounded very nervous.

"She went down to the dock. I'll get her," Susan replied.

"No, don't leave. I'm in a rush. Tell her I checked with a lady I know at the bureau. She's Andrew Dillinger's private secretary, very high up on the pole. They either don't know a thing about Golosov and Dan Ogilvy, or were stone-walling me. My guess is they're completely in the dark."

"Then Ogilvy isn't working for the FBI, or they'd know."

"I got the feeling they were just dying to find out. We've got to move fast, or Dillinger will get a net out and beat me to Golosov. I'm going to cut out to the airport right now. I'll be in touch. Tell Annie to sit tight and don't rock the canoe."

When Annie returned, Susan gave her the message. "Good," Anna nodded. "I've got the boat all gassed up and ready to go for him."

"We have a name at the FBI now, Anna," Susan said reluctantly. "Mr. Dillinger. You could call him."

"Bill is on his way," Anna pointed out.

Susan didn't persist. Something in her wanted to protect Dan for as long as possible.

Mr. Scott's next call came from Albany. Susan hurried to her aunt's side to listen. "Annie, it's me. There's trouble. Somebody's following me. I wouldn't be surprised if my phone's tapped. People know the kind of work I do. I no sooner got my whirlybird in the air than I saw he was right behind me. I'm trying to lose him. Don't sit with bagels by the phone. This may take a while. I'll give you a whistle when I land at the airport. Till then, keep an eye on the Heron. *Capisce?*"

"Do hurry, Bill," Anna said.

"They haven't left?" His voice was closer to a bark than a human sound.

"No! No, they're here, but ..."

"Whew! You just sent my blood pressure up to double digits, baby. I'll be there A.S.A.P."

"When?"

"As soon as possible. I thought you were a writer!"

The phone clicked and Anna gave a snort of impatience. An hour later, Bill called again, from some place called Johnstown. Every call sent Susan's blood racing faster. She couldn't decide which was worse; the waiting, or the phone calls.

"This bastard is sticking closer than feathers to a wet hen, Annie. I'm renting a car and going to lose him on the back roads," Scott said.

A long two hours passed. Anna busied herself with some gardening, but Susan found she couldn't do anything but sit and wait, and worry. When the phone rang again, Anna snatched it up and Susan listened in. "I'm in some dump called Poland," Scott reported.

"Poland! What are you doing in Poland?" Anna and Susan exchanged a distracted look.

"Not *that* Poland. This one's a general store, two houses and a gas pump that doesn't have a road map. But I think I've lost the shadow. You'll be hearing from me as soon as I find my way out of the woods and can rent a whirlybird. Any word on the Heron?"

"Still here. He's growing a beard, but he's still here."

Susan got a map and she and Anna scoured it till they found Poland, a mere dot, and well removed from Windmill Island. As the afternoon wore on, further calls came in from the Adirondacks, Fulton Chain Lakes and some place called Big Moose. On each occasion, Scott assured them he was hurrying toward the island at top speed.

Between calls, Anna and Susan took turns using the binoculars to see that Dan and Golosov didn't leave the island.

Susan looked at the bouquet of roses Dan had given her and drew a fretful sigh. "At this rate we're going to end up having to attend that barbecue Dan's preparing," she warned her aunt.

"It's incredible that a famous private investigator can't elude a shadow."

"I wonder who's following him. He mentioned his phone might be tapped."

"Obviously it's Russian spies. Washington is full of them, and Bill handles some very important clients."

"I wonder if Jed has seen any action from the north side of the island," Susan said listlessly. The day seemed an eternity. There was nothing as desolating as waiting for something dreadful to happen. And after it happened, her whole life would be one long regret.

"I can't sit still any longer," Anna said. "I'm going to take the *Stella Maris* over and check. You'll have to stay here to listen for the phone. I won't be gone long. If Bill calls, tell him I'll meet him at Westburg. My gun's in the cabinet drawer, if you need it."

"You'd better go around the west end of the island so Dan doesn't see you leave."

Anna left, and Susan sat on alone, staring at the dying roses and thinking.

At Dan's cottage Golosov drew out an antique watch and frowned at it.

"It's four-thirty," Dan said. "It's taking Dillinger a long time to get here. He's chasing some trouble-making private agent that might cause a lot of bother. I don't know how the man got wind we're here, unless our neighbors called him."

Golosov gave a gruff answer.

Dan worried that the ladies would be arriving for dinner in a couple of hours, and he didn't even have a steak in the house. He'd better go over there and make some excuse. Maybe he could find out what was going on. This game of cat and mouse was getting on his nerves.

He didn't want to tell Golosov the truth: with so many people knowing he was here, every reporter from L.A. to New York would be hiring boats to scout out the island and try for an interview. Until the government had arranged a new identity and safe accommodations for Golosov, he had to be kept under tight wraps. Russia would be making every effort to find him and get him back. The loss of a top scientist was a blow to their prestige, as well as to science. In fact, Russia might very well prefer to see Golosov the victim of a fatal "accident" than to see him a defector.

"Keep an ear on the phone, Zin. I'm going next door for a minute."

As Dan strode along the beach, he concluded that Anna must have notified Scott. She wouldn't have done that unless she'd thought he was doing something illegal. He still smarted under Susan's question "Whose government?" Was that what she thought of him? He didn't think they'd seen Golosov—the poor man had hardly stuck his nose out the door—but Anna's hyperactive imagination had concocted some treachery on his part, and he wanted to explain as much as he could to Susan.

Susan thought she'd be frightened when she recognized Dan coming along the beach toward Sans Souci, but she wasn't. She was too numb. She only felt a heaviness on her chest and a sick feeling in the pit of her stomach. She knew he didn't suspect they knew anything, so he had no reason to harm her. What could he want? As a precaution she told Nell he was coming, but she wasn't afraid of him.

She went to the porch and unlocked the door before he arrived, so that he wouldn't know they were keeping it locked. She even attempted a smile.

"Hello, Dan. I thought you'd be home marinating our dinner or something."

"I feel like a piker," he admitted, "but I've come to postpone dinner."

"Oh? Is something the matter?" She noticed Dan looking at the rattan settee and decided it would be safer to talk in the living room in case she needed the gun. She found it incredible that she should think of Dan and protection in the same context.

"Why don't we stay here?" he said. "It's more private."

"Anna won't bother us. She's upstairs." The lie reminded her of the first night she'd met Dan. Her instincts had been right. He *was* dangerous. She knew she should be frightened of him, but fear was an emotion, not a thought, and the emotion wasn't there. It seemed when you loved someone, you couldn't fear him.

They went into the living room and sat side by side on the sofa. Even that didn't frighten her. Dan seemed to be preoccupied. His brows were drawn together in a frown of concentration, and he hardly looked at her.

"Why are you reneging on dinner?" she prodded him.

Dan looked at her and smiled, but his eyes still looked troubled. He reached out and took both her hands in his. His warm, strong fingers closed tightly over hers. A little frisson of fear crawled up her spine—just a little one. She gazed at him, and the fear subsided.

"Susan, I'm going to tell you something, and I'd prefer you not go into any details with your aunt or anyone else. I've already told you I'm doing some work for the government here. It's a scientific experiment involving solar energy."

Susan made a determined effort to be critical. She'd forget the glow in his eyes, his hands tightly holding hers, and listen. "Doesn't the government usually conduct its secret experiments in the desert or somewhere away from populated areas?"

"Yes, usually. But we didn't want a desert for this experiment."

"I'd think the desert would be an ideal location for solar energy."

"Under normal circumstances it would, but we don't want ideal conditions. We want fairly adverse conditions, in fact. Solar energy is perfectly safe, and the sun is an endlessly renewable source, but it's very inefficient. Solar cells are only about five percent efficient. What I'm working on increases that percent to nearly ninety."

"And that's what you were doing on the cliff?"

"I've been choosing the location for the panels, yes."

Those panels in his study *could* be solar panels, she reflected. "Why on earth did you choose Windmill Island for the project?"

"With all its red tape the government moves at the speed of a glacier, and I'm in a hurry." Dan didn't add that his hurry involved spiriting Golosov away from the Russian contingent of scientists on a moment's notice. Golosov had never intimated he meant to defect, until after the meeting. The man's whispered words had come like a bolt out of the blue. What alternatives had he had? Dan thought. No one knew he'd bought half of this island for his own experiment. It had seemed the ideal spot—until Miss Milton and her niece had turned up. But he still hoped they didn't know that Golosov was with him.

"We wanted a northern location, but not Arctic," he continued. "This is about as far north as you can get in the continental U.S. The fact that it's a private island provides some isolation. All we need is the eastern end. Our information was that Anna seldom comes here. It's too bad she chose this summer. We tried to buy her out, but you know about that."

"Who is Sun Inc.?"

"It's a company I formed initially. Now it's backed by the government. I wanted to do it myself, but a professor doesn't make that kind of money. I am a professor, on sabbatical."

Susan didn't ask where he was on sabbatical from, and she noticed he didn't tell her. She didn't want to ask him directly about Golosov, either. "Are you working all alone on this? It sounds like a big project."

"Workmen will be coming in to get up the panels. I'll oversee it and attend to the electronics."

"That won't remain a secret very long." She saw the wary look descend over his features, and she thought of the gun resting in the drawer.

"It won't take long. It's just a small, pilot project." Dan smiled sadly. How strange, he mused, that he should be talking about Project ISE at this critical period in their relationship. "A few fishermen and boaters from Westburg will wonder what's going on. By the time rumors leak out, the operation will be underway and we'll know whether or not it's a success. But for the next while I'd appreciate your cooperation."

"Why are you telling me this?"

"Because you already know something irregular is going on here, and I don't want you to think I'm some sort of—" he hunched his shoulders "—bad guy. I should have worn a white hat, huh?"

Susan attempted a smile. "Yeah," she said, but her voice betrayed her mistrust.

Dan studied her thoughtfully. "You asked a rather peculiar question this morning. 'Whose government?' you said. What did you mean by that crack?"

Susan felt a ripple of fear as he stared, waiting for an answer. She'd been wrong, then. You *could* fear the person you loved. She'd always heard self-preservation was the strongest instinct. Her throat felt dry, and her cheeks were hot. She noticed the name Golosov hadn't cropped up in this sudden outpouring of explanation. The panels in Dan's playroom did support the solar energy idea, but who was going to benefit from this new technology? If the States was paying for it, why was a Russian scientist taking part? If Dan was a traitor, why didn't he just go to Russia with Golosov?

By remaining in America, he was privy to all sorts of other new scientific developments, of course.

Maybe the idea was for him to pass them all along to his new friends.

"Well?" Dan prompted her.

Susan realized he was waiting for an answer. She could hardly remember the question. *Whose government?*—that was it. She gave an unconvincing laugh. "I guess I've been associating with Anna for too long. She makes a mountain out of every molehill." She was relieved that Dan seemed to accept it. His frown became a tentative smile.

"I have no objections to being a mountain, but I don't think I'm flattered at being called a molehill. Do you think you can convince Anna to keep quiet, without telling her what it is she's not telling? What I mean is, I'd rather she not ask questions or spread any rumors of unusual goings-on here on the island."

He might as well ask the wind not to blow, Susan thought, but Dan had no way of knowing her aunt's nature. "I'll see what I can do."

He moved closer, looking toward the staircase. He thought Anna was upstairs and might come down at any moment. "Why don't we go out for a little walk?" he suggested.

"Anna's having a rest. I told her I'd mind the phone. She's expecting an important call from her publisher."

"A new book on its way?"

"An auction for paperback rights to the last one," she said, inventing on the spot. "Well, I'd better tell Nell she'll have to cook tonight after all."

She looked expectantly at Dan, waiting for him to leave. "Walk me to the door?" he asked.

He was going to kiss her, she realized. "Can't you find the way?" she parried, and pointed to it.

Dan rose and pulled her to her feet. "Lazybones. A hostess should be more gracious. Just because I'm not feeding you doesn't mean you can treat me like an unwelcome visitor."

He opened the door to the porch and pulled her into his arms. He held her so tightly that she could hardly breathe. His lips assaulted hers in a bruising kiss, and her foolish body reacted as it always did to Dan Ogilvy; it melted into submission. They shared just one quick, very passionate kiss, then he released her.

"That'll have to do you until—until I see you again. I hope it won't be too long, Susan." His smile was rather wistful, she thought.

Dan walked quickly toward the outside door, then ran along the beach toward his cottage. Susan stood watching him through the screen.

Chapter Ten

Anna returned from her boating expedition and reported that all was quiet on the northern shore.

"Dan was here," Susan told her. "We've been disinvited from dinner."

"Thank God for that! Did Bill call?"

Susan was relieved her aunt didn't ask any more questions about the visit. She was uncertain of just how much she should tell and decided that she wouldn't say anything till she'd had time to sort it out in her own head. Of course, she'd tell Bill Scott, if he ever got here. He'd know whether any of what Dan had said was true.

The next call from Bill didn't come till six o'clock. By that time Nell was busy making an emergency dinner of sandwiches while Anna and Susan had a drink on the porch. They both darted to the phone.

"Complications, Annie," Susan heard Bill tell her aunt. "I'll be a little late. These guys stick closer than Velcro. You'll have to man the fort on the island. And don't let Golosov leave! But don't terminate him, of course. Use heat if necessary. You *do* have heat?"

"It's eighty degrees here, Bill. Oh, you mean a gun! Yes, I'm . . . packing heat. Where are you?"

"I'm at some dump in the middle of nowhere. It must have a name. Wait, and I'll ask the clerk." Reception was so good that even Susan could hear the phone booth door squawk open. The next sound they heard was more ominous. Only an echo came through the wire, as though Bill had left the phone. "Hey, you guys! Let go of me. What the hell—" The snarling voices shouting at Bill were too far from the phone for Susan to make out any words, but they sounded extremely menacing.

"Bill! Bill, are you there? What's happening?" Anna demanded.

The click of the receiver being hung up sounded lethal, like the cocking of a pistol. "They've got Bill!" Anna said. "The Russian agents have caught him."

They exchanged a blank look. "We don't even know where he was calling from," Susan said. "Bill dialed direct, too, so the call would be hard to trace, maybe impossible." She stared dumbly at the phone.

"Oh, dear!" Anna began turning in circles.

Susan steeled her nerves. "Now, Anna, don't panic. You've always prided yourself on your cool head. You've assassinated princes and potentates before now."

"In real life it's different."

Susan saw that her aunt was trembling from head to toe.

"Help—we obviously need help," Susan said firmly. "But to bring F.B.I. agents in would take hours.... We'll have to notify the police from Westburg."

"Perhaps you'd better make the call, Susan."

While they were discussing what Susan should say, the phone rang again, and she answered it.

"Scott here," he said. I've got to talk to Annie."

Susan blinked in astonishment and said, "It's Bill."

Anna grabbed the receiver. "Bill! How did you escape?" As usual, Susan listened to Bill, her head close to Anna's.

"I got tired of running and decided to let them catch me. The dopes tried to take me at a phone booth in a shopping mall. As soon as they laid a hand on me, I yelled 'Help, muggers!' at the top of my lungs, and five teenagers were all over them like fleas on a dog. I gave them the slip and drove on. I'm at some place called Morristown. Is that anywhere near your island?"

"You're practically here. Drive two miles west to Westburg, and I'll be waiting for you."

"I better continue the trip solo. You might be followed if you leave the island. I'll hire a boat and drive over."

"I'll meet you on the west end of the island—they won't see you land from there."

"Which end is west?" Bill asked.

"The one where the sun is setting, Bill. Didn't they teach you about the sun at FBI school? Not the end where the windmill is, the other one."

"Right. I should be there in thirty minutes. Make that forty-five. I'll stop to buy a fishing rod and funny hat as a cover."

Anna hung up and shook her head. "Well, he got away from the Russian spies. He'll be here in forty-five minutes. I'm going to meet him."

To Susan the wait seemed hours long, but in thirty minutes Anna left for the west end of the island. Half an hour later she returned, and Susan was introduced to Bill Scott, a middle-aged man who looked seriously overweight. To his disguise of a fishing rod and funny fisherman's hat he'd added a flowered shirt and blue jeans that were, incredibly, too large for him. His graying hair was tousled when he removed the hat and his face was red from his day's exertions, but his blue eyes were cunning, and his movements were swift and smooth despite his girth.

"I think the first priority is for me to get a look at Golosov," Bill said. "Not that I doubt your word, ladies. I just want to pleasure these old eyes with a sight of him."

"We can hardly go peeking in windows in broad daylight," Susan pointed out.

"We'll have to wait till dark," Anna agreed. "Since you probably haven't eaten, Bill, I hope you'll join us for a snack. I'm afraid it's just sandwiches."

Bill consented with pleasure and wolfed down more than half the plate while Anna outlined what had been going on at the island. "I haven't had a bite since my breakfast this morning—a prune Danish and coffee," Bill said.

Anna decided half a sandwich was enough for her and placed another one on his plate. Susan hardly said anything as she sat doodling with her food, thinking of Dan. What was going to happen? "Will they arrest Dr. Ogilvy?" she asked Scott.

"It sounds like he's working for the Russkies," he replied. "After we've taken the pair of them, we'll call in the FBI. Too bad Dillinger won't be in Washington. Wouldn't I love to hear him squawk when I make the report."

"Who's Dillinger?" Susan asked.

"A big cheese FBI."

"Why won't he be there?" Anna asked.

"He's probably cooling his heels in the clink for hassling me."

Anna stared. "What are you talking about, Bill?"

"I told you—I hollered 'Muggers,' and some kids grabbed him. He had Blaine with him."

"Are you telling me it was the *FBI* that were chasing you?" she asked, aghast.

"Who did you think it was?"

"We thought it was Russian agents!" Susan exclaimed. "Oh, no, Anna. We'll be arrested. I told you you should call the police."

"Don't worry," Bill said, gloating. "Dillinger hasn't got a clue where Golosov is hiding out. The Bureau will be so glad to have the case solved for them they won't do anything but thank us. And don't think it will do our careers any harm."

Anna, convinced by the last, happy thought, wouldn't hear of Susan calling the police or the FBI or anyone official.

Until darkness began to close in, they sat around, discussing what they should do. At that time Nell came running into the living room. "There's a boat landing at the Quinns' dock!" she exclaimed.

They all ran to the screened-in porch and stared at the big white launch. "It's a Coast Guard boat!" Bill said. "Now what the devil is the Coast Guard doing here?"

Susan noted that the two men disembarking looked impressive. They wore suits, and one of them carried himself with a military air.

"God only knows," Anna replied. "Ogilvy's as sharp as a tack and as crooked as a corkscrew."

The Coast Guard boat and skipper remained at the dock.

"Let's go around by the back path and look in Dan's window," Susan said.

The three crept up to the window where Susan and Anna had seen the equipment stacked against the wall the night before. The window was closed tonight, but the shade was up a few inches. The stocky man chewing on a cigar stump was undoubtedly Golosov. He was with Dan. The Coast Guard men were beyond Susan's view, but they were obviously in the room, as Dan and Golosov often looked off to the side when speaking.

Susan caught Bill Scott staring, a beatific smile on his face. It was really Golosov! he marveled. While he withdrew from the window and discussed it in low tones with Anna, Susan kept staring at Dan. It was the last time she would see him, and she didn't intend to watch him being led away in handcuffs. Her heart felt like a lump of lead in her chest, and her jaws ached from holding back the tears. Dan was smiling—how could he bear to smile?—shaking Golosov's hand and talking to the other men. She noticed a battered leather suitcase on the floor. Suddenly Dan reached down and picked it up.

"Golosov and the men from the Coast Guard are leaving!" she said. "It looks like Dan's staying."

"Stop them!" Anna ordered.

"They're all moving out of the room into the hall-way," Susan said.

There wasn't a minute to think. Scott quickly waved the women back and took up a post to the right of the doorway with his gun drawn and pointed. When the men came out, Dan and Golosov were in front. The two men behind were just shadows.

The leave-taking seemed friendly, Susan thought.

"I'm sorry you have to go, Zin," Dan said. "We'll keep in touch. I'll let you know the results as soon as I have some data."

Golosov shook Dan's hand, then wrapped him in a bear hug.

"I'll see you in Moscow," Dan said.

Scott made his move then. "Okay, guys, hold it right there!" he called, and stepped out from the shadows, holding his gun steady.

Dan dropped the suitcase and pulled Golosov behind him. One of the Coast Guard men peered into the shadows and called. "Who's that? Is it the cops?"

Scott uttered a surprised expletive.

"Scott! You—" The Coast Guard man lunged out past Golosov.

Susan saw the second man's hand move surreptitiously to his pocket, certainly going for a gun. She heard her aunt fire a warning shot well over every-one's head. Things happened quickly after that.

Bodies seemed to be flying around Susan as she stared, horrified. The two men who had come in the boat tackled Scott. Bodies were rolling on the ground, but the one she was most interested in was Dan, and he had disappeared, along with Golosov. They must have gone back into the cottage, she thought.

They were escaping, and she couldn't attract anyone's attention to stop them! She ran toward the back of the cottage, deciding that that was where they would sneak out, and she meant to be there to meet them. She moved silently, hiding in the shadows as she ran the few yards to the rear of the house. The door was just opening. When she saw that Dan was laughing, something inside her snapped. A man who could laugh about espionage was a fiend.

"This way, Zin," he said. "We'll borrow Anna's boat and get you safely out of this madhouse."

At least they weren't armed, she thought. But she needed a weapon to stop them. A rock or fallen branch was the best she could hope for. In the light coming from the kitchen window she saw a stout fallen branch and pulled it toward her with her foot. Grasping it in her hands, she leaped out.

"Think again!" Susan said grimly, and made a swipe at Dan with her weapon.

Dan ducked and stared at her, disbelieving. "Susan!"

"Miss Knight to you."

Susan suddenly realized that her weapon was about as useful as a pillow. Dan could take it from her before she inflicted any serious damage. She felt a surge of relief when her aunt peered around the corner of the building, calling softly, "Susan."

"Bring your gun, Anna," Susan said.

"I'll get Bill Scott," Anna replied, and darted back to the front of the cottage.

Dan's hands went out in a gesture of futile incomprehension. "Put that stick down, Susan," he said gruffly.

She took a firmer grip on the branch. "You move one inch, and I'll clobber you." Her hand shook, but her resolve didn't waver. Tears slid down her cheeks.

Dan saw that she didn't hear the skipper come up behind her. He must have heard Anna's first warning shot, Dan realized. The man pounced forward and tapped her on the head with the butt of his gun. She crumpled to the ground like a rag doll.

"You idiot!" Dan yelled. "If you've hurt her...!" He rushed forward to gather Susan into his arms.

"She was threatening you!" the skipper protested.

"With a twig!" Dan pulled the branch from her limp fingers and tossed it aside. Cradling Susan in his arms, he carried her into the cottage. Her head fell against his chest, and her eyes remained closed as though she were asleep. She moaned a little when he placed her on the sofa and examined the back of her head, where a bump was beginning to swell.

Golosov had followed him, and Dan told him, "You'd better be going now, Zin. Sorry about this little incident."

Zinovi examined Susan with interest. "Pretty," he said, nodding. "But you Americans—all crazy." He said goodbye and left, shaking his head, and Dan turned his full attention to Susan.

His anger melted to chagrin when he saw her lying helpless. A tumble of black hair fell away from her pale face. She looked so young and vulnerable. She moaned at the pressure of his fingers on her sore head, and her eyes fluttered open.

Over Dan's shoulder Susan recognized his cottage, and since she was alone with him, she thought he'd won after all. The face hovering over hers was full of loving concern. His hands were gentle as he arranged a cushion under her head, but she remembered that this was the man who was betraying his country. She turned her head aside, because she couldn't bear to look at him. Hot tears scalded her eyes, but she wouldn't let them escape to show her weakness: that her heart still loved him, traitor though he was.

"Does it hurt much?" Dan asked quietly.

Her voice was filled with scorn. "Only when I laugh."

A smile slowly spread along his lips when he knew she was not badly hurt. "It is kind of funny, when you think about it."

"Funny as a rubber crutch. What now, comrade?"

Susan watched as the warmth gradually faded from his eyes, and his smile dwindled to derision. "Now I'd better go out and see if I can stop Anna from making a complete fool of herself. Don't go away; I'll be back."

Susan shook her head in confusion. Was he leaving her unguarded? He thought she was too inept to stop him, and his contempt only firmed her resolve. This was her chance to escape. Dan had left by the front door, so she decided to duck out the back and run for help. She stood, and the room turned black, but after a moment it resumed its proper shape and size and color. Her temples felt as though they were in a vice, but she could bear it. The back door wasn't locked. She went out and decided to see what was going on out front before leaving. She might be able to rescue Anna.

Her first surprise was to see that no one was holding a gun. The men were brushing dirt from their trousers as they laughed and talked in a friendly way. Anna wore a chastened air, which gave Susan a hint that her aunt had been mistaken, as usual. As Anna was making no effort to escape, Susan deduced it was safe to join her. "What happened?" she asked.

Anna attempted to laugh, but it came out a pathetic bleat. "It seems Golosov is not a spy after all. The FBI knew all along that he was here with Dr. Easton.

"You mean he's defecting?"

"So it seems. He's working on an experiment with Dr. Easton, and as the island is fairly secluded, Golosov was brought here. Solar energy experiment," she replied, and explained a few details. "And need I mention, Susan," she said with an admonishing look, "this is for your ears only."

"What has Dr. Easton got to do with Dan?"

Anna shook her head in chagrin at Susan's slowness. "He *is* Dan, Susan. I was beginning to suspect as much."

"But Cambridge told you—"

"Dr. Easton gave them a call, and they agreed to support his story," Anna explained.

As the truth began to dawn on Susan, she felt horrified at her suspicions and all the trouble she'd caused Dan. What must he think of her? He was the eminent Dr. Easton, and she'd practically accused him of being a traitor and a spy. "You said you'd met Dr. Easton. He was fat and bald," she reminded her aunt.

"I obviously got him mixed up with another scientist. I believe that other gentleman's name was Weston, not Easton. An easy mistake to make. A person in my position meets so many people."

Susan felt her insides shrink. But Dan hadn't seemed so very angry with her. "Kind of funny," he'd called it. The ice inside her melted like frost in the desert sun. Anna was babbling on, but Susan only half listened. Her eyes kept straying to Dan.

"Golosov's Russian colleagues at the meeting began to suspect he was planning to stay in America," her aunt was saying. "They tried to keep a watch on him, but apparently Golosov is powerful enough in Russia that he ordered them to leave him alone. He told Dan at the conference that he wanted to defect, and Dan helped sneak him out of the hotel that very night and brought him here. It was the only secluded place he could think of in such a short time."

"Why didn't he tell us?"

"Oh, it's all a great secret. Only the FBI knew, but I think he *might* have trusted our discretion," she said with an air of injury.

Susan, trying to understand it all, found her head reeling. "But Bill Scott said—"

"He knew nothing about it," Anna said, interrupting her. "I must say, Mr. Dillinger was rather curt about my phoning Bill." Bridling, she glared at a man, who Susan assumed was Mr. Dillinger.

Mr. Dillinger joined Anna and Susan, smiling apologetically. "I hope you can forgive any foolishness I might have uttered in the heat of battle. I didn't recognize you," he said to Anna. "I should have. I'm a Milton fan. Your photographs don't do you justice."

"We were all a little upset," Anna conceded gracefully. "As a good citizen, I felt I had to notify someone what was afoot here. It happens I have no contacts in the FBI."

"I hope that in the future you won't hesitate to call on me if any little thing should arise."

Anna accepted Dillinger's business card. Susan knew her aunt would add him to her list of contacts. Anna explained, "When Dan said he'd see Golosov in Russia, we hardly knew what to think."

"The annual meeting of the new scientific conference will be held there next year. It was in all the papers," Dillinger said.

"Ah, I've been abroad. I hadn't heard."

"We'll keep Golosov under wraps until we get him safely established with a new identity." He turned to Bill Scott. "And as an ex-CIA man, Scott, you realize none of this has happened."

"If you'd told me, we could have worked together," Scott said.

Dillinger glared. "We don't work with laymen. I'll deal with you later. Your license is coming up for renewal, I believe?"

Scott smiled blandly. "Is that a threat, Dillinger? I'd better start working up my story about how I evaded two FBI agents for an entire day and ended up getting them arrested."

"You breathe one word of that, Scott—"

"I can be quite forgetful—as long as my license is renewed with no trouble."

Dillinger grunted his assent. He and his assistant accompanied Golosov to the Coast Guard vessel. Bill Scott remained behind.

Susan looked at Dan, trying on his new name. She had already become a fan of Dr. Philip Easton. She liked his philosophy, and she loved his smile, which had often turned to her during the past few minutes of the evening.

"You should have told us, Dan," Anna said.

"My orders from the FBI were to tell no one." Dr. Easton, who was still called Dan intermittently over the next while, said, "I owe you ladies a dinner. How about it?"

"We've already eaten," Susan said. She felt embarrassed and uncertain in her relationship with Dan now.

"Will you join me for a drink at least? I feel bad about my inhospitable treatment. Let me make it up."

"Come to Sans Souci instead," Anna said. "The Quinns' cottage is a dump. Why don't you stay with us instead, Dan? For the summer, I mean. There's loads of room, and Nell is a good cook."

"Thanks for the offer, but I'm using my cottage to store my equipment. I can't abandon it."

"Come for a drink anyway," Anna persisted.

He looked uncertainly at Susan, and she smiled encouragingly. "I'd love to," he said.

Susan prepared drinks, and Anna proposed a toast to Dan's project before leaving. "To the success of Project ISE, Dan."

"I'll drink to that."

Dan went on to explain his project in some detail. He was on the verge of implementing a new solar energy system that was vastly more efficient than previous ones. It would be useful in countries with no hydroelectric facilities and avoided the danger inherent in nuclear reactors. "Golosov and I had been corresponding, so when he defected, I brought him here, thinking we'd be alone."

His smile lingering on Susan told her he wasn't entirely unhappy with the outcome, however.

Bill gave Anna a meaningful look and said, "Are there any of those sandwiches left, Annie?"

"How could there be, the way you were gobbling them down? Come on—I'll make you something to eat."

After they'd gone to the kitchen, Susan turned to Dan. She was glad for the privacy so that she could apologize, but she hardly knew where to begin. He made it easier by sitting beside her on the sofa and taking her hand.

"You must think Anna and I are crazy," she said with a disparaging shake of her head.

"Anna's incorrigible. I still have some hope for you. You're not working under the misapprehension that you helped in this case." The smile glowing in his eyes softened the censure.

"I would have helped, if you'd told the truth!"

"And I would have told the truth if I could have. I'm sorry, Susan, but you'll have to forgive me. I've already suffered enough. You can imagine how I felt when I saw that Coast Guard knock you over the head."

"Imagine how *I* felt, thinking you were a traitor." She emitted a sigh of regret. "Well, it's all over now."

His fingers moved up her arms, tightening their grip. "The fat lady hasn't sung yet."

"This isn't the opera."

"Sure it is, in the true sense of the word. Opera's just Latin for works. I still have plenty of work to do."

"There's one thing I want to know. Were you peeking in the window the first night I came here?"

"Guilty as charged. I wanted to see who was next door. I also wanted to see if you'd sent someone to fix the generator. Zinovi went scouting and found it while I was out. You were quick to notice the generator couldn't fix itself. I knew right away you were going to be trouble."

His gaze, lingering on her pale face, showed no sign of disapproval, she mused.

Dan had to make an effort to draw himself back to attention. He had the strange sensation he was drowning in the blue depths of her eyes. "How long have you known Golosov was here?"

"Anna spotted him the night she arrived. Of course, we didn't know who he was till we saw his picture in a magazine. We only knew you weren't telling the truth," she added with a questioning look.

"And you still agreed to go on seeing me?"

"We had to find out what you were doing," she explained.

"Here I thought I'd bowled you over with my charm. Did you see my wallet in my pocket the day I 'forgot' to bring it with me? I was afraid the customs men would call me Mr. Easton. Is that what caused your headache?"

"I felt the wallet when I picked up your jeans just as we were leaving the island."

Dan set down his glass and curled a strand of her hair around his finger. When he spoke, his voice was husky. "You're observant. I wouldn't have noticed if an elephant had come charging out of the bush. I was distracted that afternoon. I wanted to..."

She looked him directly in the eye. "Then why didn't you?"

"Because we were soon going to be parted, without your even knowing who I was. I didn't want you to get the idea I was some fly-by-night guy. You might have spent the rest of the summer hating me."

"Is that why you didn't..." She should have followed her own instincts, she reflected. In her heart she had known all along he loved her.

"Partly. You'd also just claimed a disinterest in marriage." With his inflection he made it a question. His eyes betrayed a sharp interest in her reply. "I don't make love with just any princess who comes along. I'm looking for a firm commitment. You'd have more time for your writing than you have working with Anna. I'd be away most of the day."

As if any of that mattered! she thought. As if anything mattered except being with him, knowing he loved her.

Before she could form an answer, Dan spoke on eagerly. "Susan, I'm sorry about all the lies and subterfuge and the unpleasant way we met. I wish it could have happened at a better time, on a real enchanted island, but the important thing is that we did meet."

Tears of joy clogged in her throat. Dan looked at her uncertainly. "That's two or three times I've apologized," he pointed out. "I thought love was never having to say you're sorry."

She felt joyful as she turned to stare at him. Dan, Dr. Easton—what was in a name? It was the man she loved, and his gentle expression betrayed the same feeling. The word *love* hung in the air between them.

She took his hand, which was still in her hair, and placed it against her cheek. He patted it, then moved to feel for the bump on her head.

"Does it hurt much?" he asked.

Her headache was gone, she realized. Magically dissipated about the time she learned Dan was innocent. "Not even when I laugh."

"I like to see you laugh," he murmured as he trailed his lips along her cheek. "Dillinger's going to make Anna another offer for the island. He wants it vacated for the continuation of my experiment. Anna will have to leave."

Engrossed in the message of his caress, Susan didn't understand his words for a minute. When they finally sank in, she turned her head and encountered his waiting lips, which seized hers in a searing kiss. His arms closed around her tightly, crushing her mercilessly against him. The next moment was a frenzy of kisses and exploring and touching. She must have misunderstood him, she thought. He couldn't have said . . . She pulled back. "Dan?"

"Mmm . . ." He nuzzled her ear and said, "The name's Phil. I've wanted to hear you say it. Maybe I can talk Dillinger into letting you stay, if you can talk me into it."

"That's blackmail!" Her voice was breathless. His teeth nipping at her earlobe did strange things to her vocal cords. They also made her feel like hot fudge inside.

"That's not blackmail. It's friendly persuasion." Then his lips assaulted hers again, and the fudge began boiling. She moved her head aside.

"Keep talking," he said in a ragged voice. "The best way to keep you here is by making you my wife. Interested?"

She found herself drowning in his gaze. She couldn't marry him so soon. She hardly knew him. Yet in some instinctive way she felt she had known him forever. She'd loved him even when she'd thought he was a traitor. Now that she knew he was her philanthropist friend, Dr. Easton, she didn't have to worry about his character. And it was unthinkable that they should be parted, just when all their other difficulties were smoothed away.

"Mrs. Easton," she said dreamily. "It sounds good to me."

Dan's worried frown eased to a smile. "I take it that's a yes?" he said, and kissed her again before she could reply.

At that inopportune moment, Anna appeared at the door. "Coffee, anyone?"

Two dreamy pairs of eyes looked at her in dismay and she turned to Bill. "I don't think they're interested in coffee at the moment, Bill. Tell me more about that forgery case you mentioned. How exactly did Fingers Malone bleach the one dollar bills before turning them into twenties? I always like to make my books authentic."

She returned to the kitchen table, and in the next room, Susan convinced Phil Easton that she should be allowed to remain on the island.

* * * * *

COMING NEXT MONTH

#622 A MAN CALLED TRAVERS—Brittany Young
City sophisticate Eden Sloane never dreamed she'd love the great
outdoors...until she met rugged Australian cattle rancher
Jack Travers.

#623 COURTNEY'S CONSPIRACY—Christine Flynn
Vivacious Courtney Fairchild and reserved Steven Powers had
conspired to make a match between their lonely relatives. But
then they discovered that their *own* match might be made
in heaven....

#624 LORD OF THE GLEN—Frances Lloyd
Nicola Sharman wanted the scoop on the mysterious lord of a
Scottish manor, but Angus McPherson, his dashing gamekeeper,
gave her heart a story worth writing home about!

#625 HEART OF THE MATTER—Linda Varner
Pediatrician Prescott Holter was looking for the perfect wife, and
Dallas Delaney was too fun-loving for such a serious job. So why
couldn't he stop thinking about her?

#626 WILD HORSE CANYON—Elizabeth August
They married out of obligation, and their families had feuded for
generations, but could feisty Maggie Randolph and irresistible
Joe Colbert forge a bond of love for the generations to come?

#627 THE PASSIONS OF KATE MADIGAN—Suzanne Forster
On the outside, police academy drill instructor Kate Madigan was
tough, but her new recruit—dark, intriguing Ty Raphaell—knew
he could reach her hidden passion....

AVAILABLE THIS MONTH:

#616 TO MARRY AT CHRISTMAS
Kasey Michaels

#617 AFTER THE STORM
Joan Smith

#618 IF DREAMS WERE WILD HORSES
Adeline McElfresh

#619 THE KERANDRAON LEGACY
Sara Grant

#620 A MAN OF HER OWN
Brenda Trent

#621 CACTUS ROSE
Stella Bagwell

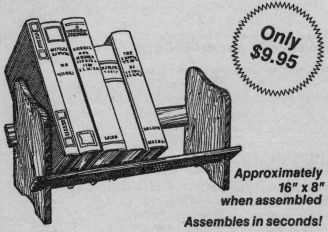